THE *Scoundrel* SEEKS A WIFE

THE SCOUNDREL SEEKS A WIFE

BOOK THREE OF *THE GARDEN GIRLS* SERIES

JEMMA FROST

Copyright © 2022 by The Arrowed Heart

Edited by Hazel Walshaw
Cover Design by The Arrowed Heart
E-Book ISBN: 978-1-955138-08-6
Paperback ISBN: 978-1-955138-22-2
First Printing, 2022

ALSO BY JEMMA FROST

Charming Dr. Forrester
All Rogues Lead to Ruin
An Earl Like Any Other
The Scoundrel Seeks a Wife
A Gentleman Never Surrenders

Dedicated to the quiet strength of introverts.

PROLOGUE

1872 LONDON, ENGLAND

The marquess was about to lose.

Clarke Calloway knew it.

As did every other player at the table.

The only person unaware of his misfortune was the marquess himself—a consummate gambler with more streaks of bad luck than good. Rumor had it he'd lost his vast family fortune, and creditors nipped at his heels.

"Call," Clarke said, eyeing the older man whose cravat revealed the dark stain of sweat around his neck.

I have him now.

Known in certain social circles for his skill with cards and women, Clarke was no stranger to struggling lords who couldn't win a game of vingt-et-un if their life depended on it, and in truth, they were his favorite people to play against.

Besting the nobility? Collecting their coin as easily as checking his pocket watch?

Well, he couldn't resist the smug pleasure it brought him.

The dealer flipped over the next card, and the Marquess of Linton groaned—his defeat written in the upturned faces laid out on the green bombazine. Grinning, Clarke clucked his tongue and accepted his winnings. One thousand pounds. Not too shabby for a night's work. Not that he made a career off the backs of blue bloods, but it padded his coffers quite nicely.

"Good game, Linton." *Thank you for being such a deplorable player.*

"Ah, yes. Same to you, Calloway." Linton swiped a handkerchief over his forehead and nodded absent-mindedly before leaving the table, no doubt to find another game to lose. The rest of the men stretched or took the time to have their glasses refilled before the next round of play began, and Clarke felt the prickling of impending... *something*.

"Are you finished yet, lovey?" Marissa leaned over his back, her arms wrapping around his shoulders to slip inside his jacket. One of the regular women Martin's offered to their patrons, she'd warmed his bed multiple times in the past, though it'd been a while since he'd frequented the upstairs quarters of the gambling hell.

"Not quite." He stood from the table and considered the room. "I've got a feeling there's more in store for me tonight besides fucking. Might want to find someone else for the evening."

A certain energy crackled in the air. He couldn't properly describe it, but had learned over the past three decades of his life to trust his gut when the sensation arose. His mum even likened it to a guardian angel keeping careful watch over her son—guiding his path—though he doubted God spent much time assigning angels to men like him. Nevertheless, Clarke heeded its warning, remaining downstairs to see if he couldn't sniff out the source of his wariness.

Marissa harrumphed, crossing her arms over an ample bosom that swelled past the neckline of her dress. "Suit yourself. But don't come crawling to me later when you're wanting a little slap and tickle." She sashayed away, and Clarke shook his head in amusement.

Not bloody likely.

Women didn't make him crawl.

They came begging for him.

Not that he could blame them. Lady or harlot, he fucked them all—ensuring their pleasure as well as his own. It was the lone gentlemanly quality he possessed in an otherwise scoundrel existence.

Nearing the bar at the back of the room, Clarke overheard someone bragging about his daughter, listing her fine qualities like she was a horse for sale at Tattersall's. "I'm telling you, Iris is beautiful, a Diamond of the First Water. Or she would've been had I known of her existence prior to a few months ago." The words boomed from the middle of a crowd, with a few syllables becoming slurred towards the end.

Perfect, a drunk windbag.

"Beautiful," the man repeated. "And a true lady, despite her rustic upbringing. Why she'll make any man the perfect bride. What about you, Sheldon? You're searching for a wife, aren't you?"

What the devil? This lunatic really *was* trying to sell the poor chit.

"No offense, but your bastard daughter isn't the kind of wife I want."

Bastard daughter?

Intrigued, Clarke moved closer. Who thought to sell their daughter at Martin's? Let alone an illegitimate one? Polite society rarely recognized such offspring, yet this man proudly displayed the connection like a piece of gold to be bandied about.

The group of onlookers parted to reveal none other than the Marquess of Linton himself, waving an empty glass in his hand while glancing wildly from man to man. "I do take offense! Iris is a sweet girl and certainly fit to warm the bed of an old codger like you!"

"It's not her feminine charms I'm concerned with—it's her lack of legitimacy. Her tainted blood. Crow all you want about beauty and grace, I suppose there's something to be said of your current acknowledgment of her, but you won't be pawning her off on anyone of note." Cut down delivered, Sheldon left along with two other men as the crowd slowly dispersed.

Curious about Linton's intentions, that peculiar energy winding tighter around him, Clarke edged into the man's view and called for two whiskys from the bartender. "Tell me, my lord. Why are you so intent on ridding yourself of this girl if you've only just met her?"

"What's a daughter good for if not strengthening the family through marriage?"

What's she good for indeed...

Clarke scowled at the older nobleman—another prime example of society's view of the fairer sex. Clarke may not be a gentleman, but at least he respected women enough to know they had more smarts than most men of his acquaintance. "And how, pray tell, do you expect her to strengthen your family?"

Linton swayed nearer, bringing a whiff of alcohol on his breath and causing Clarke to wrinkle his nose in disgust. "Truth be told, I'm in a bit of a bind. But discovering Iris was the godsend I needed to get out of it. I'm willing to accept five thousand pounds in exchange for her hand in marriage."

The exorbitant sum momentarily stunned Clarke, who prided himself on his unshakable disposition. Five thousand pounds! He must be in deep to need that much blunt.

But does his daughter possess a golden cunt?

What man would pay such an amount for one woman?

After all, Linton should be paying his daughter's dowry to a potential husband, not the other way around.

"She may be illegitimate, but don't let that detract from her more important assets. My blood runs through her veins—the blood of Lintons from twelve generations. We're one of the oldest families in the country! If these men would pull the stick out of their arses, they'd be jumping at the chance to wed Iris. Most can't imagine marrying so well." Linton paused for a breath and downed a gulp of amber liquid from his glass. "Besides, she's a pretty girl. Quiet from what I can tell. She's a lady, I tell you, blood won out with her."

Clarke wanted to laugh in the man's face. He wanted to spin on his heel, grab Marissa, and ignore that sense of impending... *something.* Something he feared had just revealed itself in the form of Linton.

I don't need a wife.

I'm not meant to be a husband.

His mind raced through every negative reason why he should leave Linton to find some other poor sap to pay off his debts, yet the idea of nabbing a lady—even an illegitimate one—fascinated him.

You don't need a lady.

But I want one.

An arrogant part of him relished the thought of strolling through Hyde Park with an illegitimate lady on his arm. Of hobnobbing with the upper crust who'd normally turn their noses up at him—a product of a sailor and butcher's daughter—yet forced to endure his and his wife's presence because of Linton.

As if those weren't reason enough, his mother would love it. She'd wanted him to marry for a long time now, and to surprise her with a lady? Clarke could already see the smile of joy lighting her frail features.

You have the financial means to meet the marquess's ridiculous requirement.

The itch became stronger—becoming a fever pitch of awareness.

Like the time he'd decided to sell his family's legacy, his grandfather's butcher's shop, to invest the money from the sale in two risky ventures. A languishing shipping company that needed an infusion of cash to match its new owner's ideas for the future, and a collaborative effort for a luxurious hotel with a man as hungry as Clarke to make a name for himself.

Both deals proved fruitful beyond Clarke's wildest imaginings. He'd put all those years of schooling his mother insisted he have to good use, and now his financial portfolio was even more diversified. Things that never would've occurred had he ignored the odd premonition he felt to take the leap into the unknown, to trust a gut instinct rather than reasonable logic.

Let's hope my streak of good fortune continues...

"Alright, you've got yourself a deal." Clarke offered a hand to shake on it, but Linton looked confused, so he smoothly pulled back and stuffed it in his coat pocket. Praying the man remembered their conversation when sober, he continued, "I'll have a contract made stating the arrangements: you'll receive five thousand pounds upon my marriage to your daughter. If I were you, I suggest arranging said nuptials as quickly as possible... before I change my mind, or your creditors get too impatient."

He waited for a reply, amused by the assortment of expressions contorting Linton's cloudy eyes and thin cheeks. When a jovial yet slurred confirmation tumbled from the lord's lips, Clarke set his empty glass on the bar, nodded farewell, and left—seeking fresh air after such a momentous decision.

What the hell have I done?

CHAPTER ONE

A FEW DAYS LATER, HAMPSHIRE, ENGLAND

Linnets twittered around the garden where Iris Taylor hummed an accompanying song to their melody while pruning the forsythia shrubs. She loved this time of year. Spring brought fresh growth and an abundance of color, renewing the hope in her chest that life could soon change for the better.

Not that she was dissatisfied necessarily. Or lived a terrible existence.

But it was rather predictable and quiet with two of her cousins-turned-sisters wed, leaving only her and Caraway to live in the family cottage. Though not a brave adventurer like Hazel or Lily, she did dream of falling in love and starting a family of her own. Envisioned a place where she belonged.

Maybe this year.

If her younger siblings could find the men of their dreams and marry, then surely her time neared, too. She'd been patient—twenty-seven years, to be exact. Was it too much to ask for love to shine its light on her? It happened to Hazel and Lily, to all of the fictional heroines she read about. Surely, she deserved a modicum of the same happiness?

Surrounded by idyllic beauty, Iris found herself once again drifting off in a daydream, her gaze staring unseeing at the horizon, where rolling green hills met blue skies, and fantasized about the sort of man she'd wed.

Kind.

Protective.

Understanding.

Handsome... though not a requirement.

Honestly, her only true requirement of a husband would be that he loved her. And since Owen, her brother-in-law, created a trust to ensure she was free to live life as she pleased, a love match wasn't out of the question. It was just a matter of finding the right man.

Lost in imagining a mystery suitor, Iris's head snapped up with a squeak of surprise when a shadow fell over her shoulders. A stranger had entered the garden.

"Sorry to frighten you, miss." Wrinkled about the face and with graying hair, the man bowed before straightening. "I knocked on the front door, but no one answered."

"My sister is visiting the village," she said dumbly. *Probably not the wisest thing to say to a stranger.* Especially as a woman alone, without anyone else around for miles. Who knew his intentions? Scrambling to her feet, Iris dusted dirt-covered hands onto the apron protecting her dress before examining the newcomer. Fine cloth draped him from head to foot, but her careful eye noticed the slight fraying of edges, which spoke of a downturn in fortune, perhaps. *Or he prefers to wear perfectly serviceable clothing as long as possible, like any person with common sense.*

"Ah, how fortuitous! As it is with you that I must speak privately."

Brows furrowing, Iris couldn't fathom what he would have to say to her. The only people of nobility she knew were her sister Lily, and her husband, the Earl of Trent, along with his mother, the dowager countess. "Are you sure it's me you seek? Iris Taylor?"

"Quite sure. Your mother—your birth mother, that is—was Martha Kent, correct?"

Shock stiffened her shoulders. She'd been abandoned as a baby. Knew her mother had left her with the Taylors—with her aunt and uncle and cousins—to be raised as one of their own. But to hear this stranger announce the circumstances surrounding her birth rendered her speechless.

How did he know?

Easing away from him, a sense of vulnerability rose to the forefront, and Iris feared what he'd say next. "Yes, that is true. Did you know her?"

"Shall we move this conversation indoors?" He gestured to the cottage, but Iris didn't feel comfortable being alone inside with him. Not to mention the rising tide of agitation prickling her skin. No one ever talked about Martha Kent. Not villagers. Not her parents when they were alive, aside from a brief explanation of how she came to join their family.

What connection did this man have with her mother?

Why did he seek me out?

"Here is fine, sir. Please tell me what you've come to say. Why does it matter if Martha Kent was my biological mother?"

"Because I believe that makes me your father, and *I* am the Marquess of Linton." He smiled and opened his arms, as if expecting a hug of elation. As if she should be overjoyed to discover her biological father was a nobleman of the realm, making Iris a lady by blood.

The brisk March air chilled her lungs, and a slight choking sound emitted from her throat. The Queen of England could have arrived in full regalia, and Iris couldn't have been more stunned.

A father!

Well, another one, she thought, sending a prayer up for dear Papa. After two decades, the identity of the man who'd fathered her was finally revealed.

"Excuse my reticence, but how is that possible?" she asked, licking dry lips. "What makes you think such a thing?"

"When I first saw you at the Earl and Countess of Trent's wedding last summer, it became obvious. I approached the Earl about our possible familial connection, but he never brought it up again. I can only assume by your reaction that he never told you of my suspicions."

No, Owen hadn't, and the realization hurt. Both him and Lily—for surely her sister knew, too—had kept this monumental secret from her like she was too weak to handle the news. Iris's family always teased about her tiny stature and fairy-like attributes, but a delicate-looking outward appearance didn't translate to an equally delicate disposition. She was stronger than she looked.

And to keep this from her since last summer! Almost a year gone with nary a peep from either of them.

Prompted by her stunned silence, Linton removed a small cameo from his jacket pocket and gave it to her before continuing, "Of course, I have evidence of our relation. This is a portrait of my sister Agatha, who you resemble quite closely from the light blonde hair to your peculiar eyes—grey-blue turned silver. Then I remembered a long-ago affair with a country girl named Martha Kent, and when I mentioned her name to Trent, he confirmed what I believed. I can't tell you how happy I am to have found you." His arms raised again for an embrace, but she denied him, stepping further back as her mind struggled to comprehend the enormity of what he'd relayed, numb fingers tracing the delicate face of a woman who, indeed, matched Iris in coloring.

An entirely separate family.

Owen and Lily had learned her biological father wanted to know her, yet they hadn't shared the information. Why?

This man claimed happiness at her existence when most people would shun a bastard child. Why not him? A man of the peerage?

Accept him. Don't question it.

Conflicting thoughts swirled into a rushing hurricane battering Iris's mind. So many questions. So many emotions.

Yet faint hope dared to sprout in the eye of the storm. Fought to overcome the force of logic and caution.

All her life, she'd searched for belonging. Despite a loving family, she'd always felt on the outskirts after becoming an unexpected burden on their lives in infancy. So, Iris made sure to exhibit her best qualities—to be kind and polite—and to not cause trouble, due to a lingering fear of abandonment. Of not being enough since her mother left.

Linton was the answer to all of those feelings.

He wanted her.

Hadn't willfully abandoned her.

"Truly? You're not horrified to learn you have an illegitimate daughter?" She waited for his answer, a single thread of prudence holding her back from completely accepting him. Her family would suggest using more caution, but Linton didn't seem like a bad man with hope lighting his gaze. And the sight of a faint, star-shaped birthmark below his ear brought her own hand up to trace a similar mark on the side of her neck.

"I'm a widower, my dear. No children to speak of after my wife died years ago. My only regret is that we couldn't have met earlier. You're a woman now instead of a little girl."

Oh, a widower. Poor man.

Sympathy instantly softened her demeanor, and Iris finally edged close enough for their bodies to embrace in a long-overdue hug of affection. The scent of bergamot tickled her nose—*the smell of my father*—and a seed of affection grew in her chest as her arms wrapped tighter around his taller form.

They stood together under the sun for a couple of wonderful minutes before Linton dropped his arms and shuffled back. Clearing his throat, he stared at her with fondness, or at least that's what she attributed the warmth in his gaze to.

Girlhood fantasies that she'd carefully kept hidden away for years filled her mind. With her love of novels and romantic endings, Iris had imagined what it would be like for her biological father to swoop into her life, full of love and adoration. She'd dreamed of a man searching the world for his lost daughter before guilt would inevitably force her to bury those musings. Iris had a father who loved her, who took her in when he could've refused to accept a bastard child in his home.

She had no right to fantasize about another fatherly figure when her childhood was as happy as it could be with the Taylors. But was it wrong to now revel in a secret dream come true?

Iris hoped not.

"My dear, if I may be frank, there's another reason why I'm overjoyed to discover you, and I'm afraid it paints me in a rather bad light." Tugging on his sleeve, he paced in front of the shrub she'd been pruning, and a knot formed in her stomach. What else could he have to disclose? "You see, I'm in financial trouble. These men—disreputable bounders, I assure you—are threatening to harm me if I don't repay a sum they claim I owe them."

Her eyes widened at the similarity of their stories. Only last year her family was threatened by a Mr. Laramie who claimed their deceased father owed him money. He would've taken the cottage if not for Owen stepping in. Then Laramie spiraled into an obsessive frenzy—almost killing Owen and a pregnant Lily.

"It's a steep amount. Five thousand pounds, if you can imagine it, and they're determined to extract it from me. Why I've received threatening letters, a sabotaged saddle that almost saw my neck broken during a ride about Hyde Park... I can't tell you how terrifying it's been, and I fear approaching any officer of the law since they've warned me about enlisting aid. However, a possible solution has arisen. A generous man has offered to pay the horrible men and requires only one thing in return."

Worry gnawed at her gut. She couldn't let her father be hurt, too.

"How can I help? Whatever he—*you* require—I'll do what I can. I don't have much money, but maybe I can—"

"No, dear. I don't expect you to pay the ruffians." Linton chuckled at her hasty offer, patting her shoulder in a show of fatherly amusement. "However, the gentleman is young and handsome, and it didn't sit well letting him help me for nothing... So, I wonder if you might be willing to marry the man in exchange for assuming my debts. I realize it's a drastic measure, but part of a father's duty is to assure his daughter is cared for. Mr. Calloway would make an excellent husband for you while helping me at the same time. What do you think?"

Marriage!

Iris wished she hadn't stood up yet.

Dizziness set in, and she reached for Linton's arm to steady the onset of wobbly knees. "Marriage? You arranged a *marriage* for me? Without us even meeting?"

"I apologize for the hastiness, but I blame the insistent warnings from those men. I felt I had no other choice, but I truly believe the two of you would make a lovely pair. You'd be settled in London, closer to me, and have a future free of financial concern." He patted her hand kindly. "I would never force you into anything, though. I can try to figure out another—"

"No, I'll do it." She must. For her father's sake.

You don't even know the man! Either of them—father or betrothed!

But she couldn't refuse Linton, especially with his life in danger. What if she lost him so soon after their reunion?

Besides... perhaps this was how things were supposed to be all along.

Hadn't she been praying for a change? For a husband and family? Well, here they were—plopped into her lap as if God had personally delivered them.

"You... You will?" The relief that overcame Linton's entire body sealed her resolve. Already he stood a little straighter, a nimbleness about him.

"Yes. When shall we wed?" Iris would do this for her father's sake and guarantee a future where they could safely get to know one another—where they could form a true bond of familial love.

And who knows? Despite the circumstances, your betrothed Mr. Calloway could be the love of your life.

CHAPTER TWO

"**B**loody fucking hell," Clarke muttered under his breath after catching a glimpse of his bride descending a gleaming black carriage. Frozen at the church window, oxygen deserted him along with every thought in his head—a feat for someone whose mind constantly raced from subject to subject.

"Are you trying to get smite down before your vows?" William Porter, his friend and business partner, drawled from his seat once Clarke's epithet reached him. "What's caught your attention?"

"The bride."

"Hideous little thing? Buckteeth? Balding?"

Clarke nailed him with a piercing glare. "I can't marry her."

What had Linton been thinking, offering his daughter up to a man like him? In the fortnight it had taken to arrange the nuptials and retrieve a special license, he'd asked himself the same question every day, and the answer always circled back to Linton's outrageous debt.

However, surely the man could've found a more suitable husband with pockets to let than a scoundrel like him? Because the woman Clarke saw exiting the carriage dressed in cream silk and lace deserved better.

Forget his plan to impress his mother with a lady wife.

Forget hobnobbing with the elite just to spite them.

He must've had one too many drinks the night he agreed to Linton's proposal.

"I wish you would've come to that conclusion when I said the very same thing after you notified me of this scheme. Unfortunately, I'm afraid we're too far gone for you to back out now."

"Vows haven't been exchanged yet." Clarke turned to find Linton. Leaving the small retiring room they'd been sequestered to, he marched down a short hallway to another door and tried the knob. Locked. He moved to the next until one opened to the altar where Linton sat in the front pew... along with a dozen other guests.

All friends of Linton and his bride, he supposed, since Clarke's list of invitees consisted of one. Mixing his usual crowd of nouveau riche with Linton's snobby society would've been amusing, but he'd decided against it last minute. Clarke's wedding day would already be full of surprises, starting with his mysterious bride, no need to add more kindling to the potential fire.

A choice he was profoundly grateful for now that the nuptials would not be occurring.

"What the devil are you doing?" Porter hissed from behind him, and Clarke clutched his arm, shoving him forward.

"Grab Linton and bring him to me. I'm calling this whole farce off."

"Haven't you already paid the man?"

Yes, he had.

Idiot.

But Linton kept begging for funds to satisfy his creditors, even suggesting Clarke and his bride-to-be elope to Gretna

Green instead of moving forward with the hastily planned wedding her family put together. He couldn't in good conscience deny the poor woman a proper wedding with her friends and family, so Clarke had relented and paid the five thousand pounds early. Now, he regretted the decision.

For there was no doubt Linton had already spent the money.

Fuck.

Growling in frustration, he closed the door with a firm click and stomped back to the room the curate had given him to prepare for the day. Clarke caught sight of his frowning expression, hair askew from multiple runs of his hands through it, and bared his teeth at the unkempt beast glaring back.

"Good god, man! What's so terrible about the chit?" Porter asked, genuine concern inching into his voice as his friend refused to calm down. "Is she missing a vital feature? You haven't spoken with her, so we can't know the status of her wit yet. But clearly, you saw something out there to make you change your mind."

"I can't marry her," Clarke repeated, remembering the exact moment she came into view and snatched the breath from his lungs. "Because she's a damn mythical creature. A fairy sprite come to life and look at me." He swept a hand down to encompass his large form. "Do I look like someone who can handle a little sprite without breaking her the moment my hands touch her?"

Porter stared.

He swallowed.

His lips trembled.

Then, he laughed, unable to control his merriment any longer. Bending over, hands on his knees, Porter chortled loudly and for interminable minutes while Clarke debated putting the man out of his misery with a good punch to the gut.

"When you're done enjoying my misery, perhaps you could offer help? You're supposed to be my best man, after all."

Said best man wiped errant tears of mirth with the back of his hand, attempting to sober himself. "You're right, of course. I just never knew a man to bemoan his fate of marrying a beautiful woman. Only you would find it troublesome."

"I have nothing against beautiful women. It's tiny, fragile women who could snap beneath a strong breeze."

"Or your strong hand?" Porter supplied, one last laugh echoing in the room before he lifted a hand in supplication as Clarke moved to take a step forward. "I'm afraid my only advice is to handle her with care. Because you are stuck, my friend. There's no stopping this wedding unless the bride herself runs screaming down the aisle after seeing you." A speculative gleam entered Porter's eyes. "Which isn't entirely out of the question, I suppose. If her minuscule self scares you, perhaps your behemoth size will frighten her."

"One can hope." Clarke heaved a deep sigh and sank into a wooden chair, waiting for the curate to retrieve him. He didn't know what he'd expected from the woman meant to be tied to him forever. Intelligent. Pretty. Not too demanding. Those would've ranked on his list.

Their marriage wasn't a love match, and Clarke held no expectations of love or fidelity. They'd share a bed for as long as they were interested, then live separate lives like most couples.

But he couldn't just *fuck* this ethereal fairy of a woman; she'd be liable to dissolve into pixie dust.

Again, her small form came to mind. Slim ankles barely revealed as she lifted her dress. Delicate hands engulfed by the man who helped her to the ground. He hadn't seen her face, but Clarke knew it would match: dainty features incongruous with his own coarse exterior.

Organ music played—signaling the beginning of the end for him—and on cue, a knock rapped on the door, summoning them to the altar.

Porter clapped a hand on his back in encouragement while Clarke mumbled a reluctant prayer.

God help him and his little sprite.

CHAPTER THREE

I'm getting married today.
        To a man I've never met.

Iris's sisters and Owen hadn't approved of her hasty decision or Linton's abrupt appearance in her life. Apparently, as her brother-in-law and long-time friend, Owen felt he should've been involved, yet he'd relinquished his chance by not telling her sooner about her biological father's existence.

She'd listened to their arguments, kindly addressed their concerns, then continued to plan for her upcoming nuptials. Which didn't require much from her at all, aside from a wedding gown. The dowager countess, Owen's mother, had decided to take care of the details, citing her love of the Garden Girls as daughters and as such requiring a mother's touch for their nuptials.

If only the rest of the family was as accommodating, Iris mused as the conversation on the carriage ride over to the church replayed in her mind.

"First Hazel marries a stranger, and now you. Has the world gone mad?" Cara, the eldest Taylor sister, threw her hands up in annoyance and shook her head. Lily and Owen, who sat across from them, nodded in agreement but wisely kept their mouths shut.

"Jonathan was only a stranger to us, not Hazel. As Mr. Calloway is a stranger to me, but not Lord Linton. I trust his judgment." And the importance of my marriage when it comes to his safety. *She wouldn't retract her agreement to this arrangement, but she also wouldn't share the true impetus of the hasty wedding with her family.*

Because the potential outcome wouldn't endear the marquess to her family. Owen would offer to pay off the debt, thus adding another strike against Linton. And her sisters would view her father in an unflattering light for even suggesting such a deal.

No, as Linton's daughter and to show her commitment to him, she'd marry Mr. Calloway and hope for a happy ending, like in all the novels she enjoyed reading. Dreams of love and companionship could be a reality.

Good thing Lily's softened or else she'd accuse you of living with your head in the clouds... again.

"You barely know the man, Calloway or Linton. Why does everything need to be rushed?" Cara persisted. "Why not take the time to acquaint yourselves with each other? And this betrothal... It still doesn't make sense to me."

"It doesn't have to. All you need to do is support my decision." Iris smiled and reached for Cara's hand, squeezing it in affection. *Cara was practical and responsible—the sister they all relied on for her stability. It came as no surprise that she struggled with Iris's rash choice, but Iris couldn't offer her any more comfort than she already had.*

"We support you. We just don't want to see you hurt," Lily chimed in, and once again, Iris marveled at the change her marriage to Owen had wrought. Though still brash and fiery,

Lily's tough demeanor had been tempered by Owen's love and the arrival of their child, Benjamin.

"I'll be fine. I promise," she said, turning her attention outside. With a final jostling of the carriage, they rolled to a stop on the dirt path in front of the church, and Iris breathed a little easier seeing their destination. It wouldn't be long now.

Vows exchanged. Wedding breakfast partaken. Then, later, the wedding night.

A shiver of excitement ran down her spine in anticipation as she considered that particular wedded delight again.

Perhaps it was wanton to look forward to spending an evening alone with her husband, but she'd seen the way Hazel and Lily were with their husbands. She'd heard their dreamy sighs and adoring expressions as they described the marriage act to her. Obviously, it wasn't as distasteful as most young women were taught, though there would be one glaring difference between Iris's wedding night and her sisters'—the fact that her husband was a stranger, not a beloved companion.

Yet.

The walk from the carriage to the church entry passed in a daze as she yearned to meet her future husband, imagining a gentle blonde-haired, blue-eyed man before the vision morphed to red hair and freckles with a shy demeanor—the perfect pairing for her own reserved personality.

They would read by the fire in the evenings, sharing their favorite quotes. And on Sundays, they'd walk to church, then discuss the sermon afterward at a special picnic he'd fashioned just for her. Romantic scenarios abounded, and Iris let them carry her away to a dreamland void of heartache or trouble while she followed her sisters down a hall to a waiting room.

Until a slightly ajar door allowed masculine voices to drift out, pricking her consciousness.

"I can't marry her."

Iris jolted.

Surely, she hadn't heard correctly.

Pausing, she fell behind her sisters, her gut tightening in response to the harsh words. *I should walk away. I shouldn't eavesdrop.* But her potential husband had just declared her unfit to marry. At least she assumed it was him... for what other man would be present, declining to wed his bride?

Her mind and belly, a beehive of activity—buzzing bits of shock flitting about while drowning out everything except for the gravelly voice coming from the room to her left—Iris edged closer, intent on hearing her betrothed's objections.

"Because she's a damn mythical creature. A fairy sprite come to life and look at me. Do I look like someone who can handle a little sprite without breaking her the moment my hands touch her?"

Fairy sprite.

A familiar descriptor her own family used, and relief poured through Iris as the bees transformed into butterflies and migrated south. Mr. Calloway only feared harming her—doubted her strength.

This she could handle.

She would prove she was strong enough for her new husband.

She would learn to please him.

And Clarke Calloway will learn to love me.

Easing away from the doorway with a determined smile, Iris floated down the hall and into her sisters' waiting arms as they adjusted her hair, veil, and the train of her dress. Making sure everything looked perfect before they exited for her procession down the aisle.

"You are a beautiful bride," Hazel sighed in awe; she must've arrived while Iris had been eavesdropping. Everyone smiled in agreement, the four sisters barely fitting in the medium-sized mirror perched on the wall as they perused her bridal appearance.

"Thank you," Iris demurred. It was widely acknowledged in the village that she possessed the most beauty of the Taylor sisters, but it didn't bother them. Each sister held a unique charm, and they accepted their individual gifts and flaws.

"After today, there will only be one Taylor left in Shoreham," Hazel pointed out, her gaze meeting Cara's in the mirror.

Lily laughed good-naturedly. "Nice to see I don't count as a Taylor any longer."

"You're part of the Trent family, dear. I meant no offense," Hazel said, hugging her side. "What I meant was that we can focus all our efforts on seeing Cara wed next. With the plethora of gentlemen in our circles now, we should be able to scrounge someone up with no problem."

"How lovely. I've always wanted a scrounged-up husband." Cara left the group and toyed with a loose thread on her bodice. "Don't concern yourself with me. I'm perfectly content with my lot in life, especially now that I have the generous trust Owen set up for me at my disposal."

An indiscernible look passed between Cara and Hazel, as if one knew something the other wasn't saying. But it was quickly forgotten when Owen barged into the room, ushering them out to their places at the back of the church.

"It's time, ladies," he announced before extending his arm to Iris. Linton had offered to walk her down the aisle, and she'd seriously considered his proposition. But in the end, Iris could only picture Owen by her side, her brother-in-law and surrogate brother before that. He'd been a constant male presence in her life, minus his years touring the Continent, and gratitude for his friendship trumped her budding connection with Linton. It felt too intimate to give a man she'd known for two short weeks the honor—even if he was her biological father.

Five minutes later, they strolled down a petal-covered aisle to the sound of Wagner in the background, and Iris caught the first sighting of her betrothed.

Clarke Calloway.

Oh, my.

Lungs hitching in her chest, Iris's slippered feet stumbled before Owen caught her forward motion, averting disaster. The man standing next to Father Todd exuded a raw energy that encapsulated and enticed her, even from the opposite end of the church. Broad as an oak tree and seemingly as sturdy, his feet braced shoulder-width apart while his hands remained clasped behind him, he looked the epitome of a sporting man.

And former fantasies of hair color or personality faded in the wake of reality.

When she finally reached him, her head barely topped his shoulder, and a peek upward found her gaze clashing with his intense one through the gauze of her veil. Quickly diverting her eyes, a wave of heat rolled over her like she'd just stepped out into the middle of the Sahara Desert.

Father Todd began a speech about the bonds of marriage and becoming one while Iris listened with half an ear, too engrossed in the man next to her and the effect he had on her body. No Prince Charming, according to her old children's books, he more resembled the villain with his dark coloring, yet it didn't deter her.

Polar opposites in exterior—dark and light, large and small—Iris wondered if the same would hold true in other aspects of their lives.

"Do you, Clarke Evan Calloway, take Iris Katherine Taylor as your lawfully wedded wife?"

Clarke's gravel-toned affirmative resonated low in her belly, and Iris's reply came quiet but sure when Father Todd addressed her next, eager to skip to the part where she and her husband could get to know each other at long last.

The tart aroma of citrus wafted in the air, and Iris knew it emanated from him. An interesting scent for a man, considering the ones she knew preferred richer, woodsy fragrances, but the fresh bite of Clarke's intrigued—invited one to lean nearer. Inhaling deeply, a delighted smirk played about her lips. She couldn't have dreamed of a better start to their first meeting.

Her husband fascinated her.

Now, I must do the same for him.

CHAPTER FOUR

C larke knew beautiful women.

They flourished in every facet of life from the bored duchess with wrinkles beginning to appear around her eyes to the strict schoolteacher who hid mounds of curves under plain clothes to the accomplished opera singer known for her acrobatic ability in bed. He'd seen them all—clothed in silks, clothed in nothing but silky skin. If asked, he would've confirmed that beauty held no particular sway over him. Women were fine creatures in all forms.

Clarke knew this.

Then why the hell can't I stop gaping at my delicate little wife?

The moment the veil shrouding her face lifted, he'd felt like a bucking stallion had kicked him in the chest—driving out all semblance of reason or control. Because only one thought dominated his mind: tossing her over his shoulder and finding the nearest private alcove to perform all sorts of wicked acts on her delectable body.

Of course, an entire congregation of guests watched their exchanging of vows while a damn vicar prattled on before them. Would've made for quite the scandal—the groom hauling his bride away like a Neanderthal.

"Mr. Calloway, congratulations on your nuptials. You've gained a lovely bride." The Earl of Trent approached with his wife, and Clarke accepted the man's hearty handshake. *My new in-laws*. Apparently, he'd gained an entire gaggle of family members, from Iris's three sisters to their husbands.

Not to mention your greedy father-in-law.

Linton socialized with a couple on the other side of the ballroom which hosted the wedding breakfast and reception, Iris—his new wife—in tow.

"Thank you, my lord. I'm quite fortunate."

Another voice entered the conversation as Mr. Jonathan Travers and his wife Hazel joined the group. "Indeed... Although, you're no stranger to good fortune from what I've heard."

"Oh?" Clarke drawled, keeping a watchful eye on Iris. They still hadn't said more than a few words to the other, since she'd been immediately commandeered by her father upon their arrival at the breakfast. "I wouldn't put much stock in gossip."

"Not even from a mutual acquaintance?" Travers asked. "My wife and I are friends with Dr. Robert Forrester and his wife, who I believe you've met through Mr. Porter."

"Ah, yes. Fine couple. Did they regale you with the tale of how Porter and I became business partners then?" It wasn't exactly an interesting story, nothing out of the ordinary, but Porter did like to flaunt their successful venture into the hospitality sector with two booming hotels—one in London and the other in Manchester.

The conversation continued from there, thankfully upheld by the two couples, while he offered brief input every now and again, his focus completely taken by his oblivious wife.

What is it about her?

The peculiar silver eyes that had plunged into his soul upon first sight?

The sweet hum of a song that she didn't think he'd hear on the carriage ride to their wedding breakfast as Linton monopolized the conversation?

Like a siren from the depths of the sea, her fascination for him held fast, threatening to drag him under waves of obsession... and inevitable disappointment. Because he didn't care to obsess over his wife.

Didn't need another obligation.

Especially one who looks as fragile as baby's breath and just as innocent.

Noting the sudden trajectory of his wife, he straightened his posture and affected an expression of composed ambivalence.

"Calloway, I'm afraid I've stolen your wife for too long." Linton arrived with Iris, transferring her arm to Clarke, who tucked it alongside his, and their size difference glared in the room's sunlight. She was so tiny compared to him.

He mustn't break her.

Though he worried that would be easier said than done as his large hand covered her much smaller one—the delicate bones putting him in mind of porcelain or crystal, breakable and fine.

Exactly what I didn't want in a wife.

AT LAST.

Iris drifted into her husband, using their entwined arms as an excuse to be nearer. She bit her lip to hide the thrill running through her veins at being in his presence. His intoxicating scent. His low baritone voice.

Everything about him captivated her, and she wished they were alone already.

But the rest of the reception and a train ride to London lay between them and their new home. Between them and privacy. Was it too selfish to imagine everyone disappearing from exhaustion, leaving them alone together?

"Are you excited about the move to London?" Lily asked, her nose wrinkling in distaste. She'd forever be a country girl, no matter her title as a countess.

"Yes, a change of pace will be pleasant." The muted words struggled past the sudden lump in her throat, a flush traveling up her neck from the weight of Clarke's dark gaze upon her. For all her dreams of wanting to be alone, there remained a hurdle to overcome first: her shyness around him.

Because he rendered her quite speechless.

Not that she was the most rambunctious of the Taylors, preferring the background in conversations, but she'd never been completely at a loss on how to act or what to say. Even during the carriage ride from church to the Trent ballroom, she'd retreated into a favorite melody, humming quietly, while her father jabbered on.

Iris dearly wanted to speak with Clarke, but the fact of the matter was he intimidated her. Not necessarily his enormous size, though it certainly gave her pause, but his demeanor—the commanding aura surrounding him that drew everyone's attention.

Most especially those of the female persuasion, she thought worriedly. Admiring stares from women around the room hadn't gone unnoticed, and Iris feared her earlier prediction of being able to make her husband happy paled in the wake of a far more realistic outcome: his possible desire for a marriage in name only—for freedom to flit about London with another woman on his arm.

Then something terrible occurred to her as she surreptitiously studied Clarke. What if he already had another woman waiting for him in London? A mistress whom he loved? The details of why he'd chosen to pay her father's debts and marry her remained hazy, but it certainly wasn't due to affection on his part.

What if she was destined to be abandoned again?

This time by her husband?

Quit worrying before you make yourself sick!

But the terrible thought stuck with her. Through breakfast. Through farewells to her family. All the way until they stepped into their home in London—a lovely brownstone Clarke had described on the train ride while she managed encouraging nods and simple sentences. Both of them keen on sticking with safe topics rather than delving into each other's personal lives in the midst of a crowded passenger car.

"Welcome home, Mrs. Calloway." Clarke ushered her inside a grand foyer with a cherry-stained staircase ascending from the right. Bright rectangles on the wallpaper marked where framed artwork should be, the intricate design not yet dulled by time and exposure to the sun, and Iris wondered why the pieces had been removed. "I hope this is amenable to you. If not, we can always find something more to your liking."

The extravagant promise of giving up one home to so easily purchase another astounded her. Iris's life had been spent entirely in Shoreham—in their family cottage—even when Papa taught at university. They never stayed with him long-term, and they certainly couldn't afford a second home.

"This is quite alright," she said weakly, a tentative smile trembling on her lips. "Thank you."

"Oh, I thought I heard someone come in! We were preparing supper in the kitchen or else we would've greeted you upon arrival!" A short, robust woman waddled forward, hands wringing the apron at her waist before dipping into a curtsy. "I'm Mrs. Betty Franklin, the housekeeper. And this is Mr. Alistair Jones, the butler." She gestured towards a slender man hurrying to stand beside her. "Edith is upstairs ensuring the master suite is ready for the happy couple." Mrs. Franklin winked, causing roses to bloom on Iris's cheeks at the implication. "And I suppose you already met Jimmy outside. He takes care of everything out of doors, from the gardens to the horses. Oh, and Mrs. Patricia Marks is our cook; she's back in the kitchen. We're a bit short-staffed with the five of us, but we make do."

"You have my complete faith, Mrs. Franklin." Iris stepped forward and impulsively pulled the woman's dry palms into her own. The housekeeper jerked at the unexpected touch, then returned the comforting squeeze Iris gave her. "From what I can see, everything looks lovely, and I'm sure we'll be glad to hire any help you need..." Her questioning gaze caught Clarke's and he nodded, a far-off look ghosting over his amber eyes.

"Ah, I can tell we'll get along just fine, Mrs. Calloway." A warm smile softened the lines of worry around the older woman's mouth. "If the two of you would prefer to freshen up from your journey before dinner, I'll show you to your rooms, along with giving a brief tour of the home on our way?"

"That sounds lovely. Thank you." The three of them ambled through hallways and spare rooms before Iris's path diverged from her new husband's as they retired to separate chambers to change. Edith, the aforementioned maid, helped Iris remove her traveling gown and don something more appropriate for dinner—a surprisingly elegant affair, Iris discovered upon being seated at the dining table.

"Our former employer enjoyed the finest things life had to offer, including the best cuisine," Mr. Jones explained after seeing the awe written on his new mistress's face. Clarke coughed at the information but didn't elaborate, and courses continued their journey to and from the kitchen with the butler providing helpful commentary while delivering dishes until the bride and groom sat back from the table sated.

She both appreciated and loathed Mr. Jones's hovering throughout the meal. He provided welcome insight into her new home, but the constant presence of a third party prevented any real conversation from forming between she and her husband.

Finally, as the last bite of dessert settled in her stomach, Iris broached the topic foremost in her mind. "It's getting rather late... I think I'll change for... bed." Their butler discreetly disappeared as Clarke's stoic expression wore on her.

Was he not eager for their wedding night?

Probably not if you keep stuttering like a fool.

Iris berated the stammering mess she'd become, incapable of even uttering a full sentence coherently. Sighing, she muttered a hasty good evening before excusing herself and hurrying upstairs to her bedroom suite, where she again found Edith, this time turning down the blankets. "Oh, hello... Would you mind helping me with this gown? Usually, I'm self-sufficient, but this is a tad more elaborate than I'm used to." Since Lily and Owen's mother had insisted on gifting her an entire trousseau full of fashionable pieces meant for London's streets rather than the country roads of Hampshire.

The girl expertly undid the hooks and laces at the back of the mossy green dress along with helping Iris change into a clean nightgown, carrying the layers of her gown away. Once Edith left, Iris quickly ran to the trunk at the end of her bed and dug around the large chest until her hands brushed soft fabric near the bottom.

She gingerly removed the gossamer gown and thanked her sisters for their forthcoming advice about her wedding night. Hazel and Lily had both sat her down to explain what to expect before presenting this gauzy scrap of silk.

So pretty.

So bare.

Iris whipped the plain white nightgown she wore over her head and tossed it aside to shimmy into her gift—or rather, her gift to Clarke.

I hope he likes it.

I hope I don't embarrass myself.

CHAPTER FIVE

If her ethereal beauty hadn't already ensnared him, her kindness would've collapsed the trap in quick fashion.

Throughout their tour of the home with Mrs. Franklin, Iris had been sweet and encouraging, never looking down her nose at the older servant. Which he supposed made sense, considering she only recently learned of her birthright as a lady. He'd trailed behind them like a leashed puppy, hanging on her every word, searching for a flaw.

And found none.

Goddammit.

She embodied grace and poise—a lovely English rose—destined to be crushed in his bear paws.

He'd tried distracting himself with his newly acquired home. A house he'd won from another down on his luck lord at Martin's. A wife, a brownstone, and even his horse had been a debt repaid. Would these idiotic blue bloods ever learn to quit while ahead?

The quiet pattering of feet echoed from the hall, and Clarke saw the maid walk by the study he'd retreated to after supper. Because he'd needed a stiff drink. One guaranteed to calm him enough to bed his wife like a civilized man instead of a feral beast.

When she'd mentioned preparing for bed...

A rumbled growl of desire erupted from his chest. He'd almost chased her to the room himself, intent on bearing her down to the floor wherever he caught her. Common sense rallied at the last minute, though, and he'd kept himself seated. Barely.

But the time had come to perform his husbandly duty.

If his wife didn't need her maid, then that meant she needed *him*.

Swallowing the final gulp of his whisky, Clarke shuffled upstairs, careful to keep a sedate pace. To maintain control. However, when Iris opened the door shortly after his inquiring knock, another restraint snapped, and a picture of his raw-boned hands hanging onto the remaining line arose.

Silver eyes. Pale blonde hair. Pearly skin where vulnerable blue veins pulsed across her body—a body wrapped in white silk that skimmed over her soft curves. She was resplendent in the moonlight, altogether intoxicating.

I'm royally fucked.

"Good evening." She moved back to allow him entry, and the subtle scent of honey and vanilla filled his lungs.

Delicious.

Switching to inhaling through his mouth to avoid the tempting fragrance, he marched past her to the other side of the bedroom. "Good evening. I trust this room is to your liking?" Excellent. A normal, civilized question a husband might ask his wife.

Unlike, I trust you're ready for me to pound your wet cunt into the floral bedspread?

"Yes, it's more than I expected, truthfully. I'm used to sharing a room with my sisters, so this enormous space will be an adjustment." A shy smile wrapped around him and hooked into his heart. Or the near vicinity of the foolish organ.

"One that won't be too strenuous, I hope." He winked. She blushed.

Oh, hell... He wanted to see how far that particular shade of pink traveled. *Stop flirting. You're only torturing yourself.*

Clarke couldn't afford to work himself into a higher lather; he stood at the precipice as is. *Do only what's necessary—brief small talk to make her comfortable, then a gentle joining.* Two words he'd never used to describe sex before, but this proved the exception. He needed to keep things slow and tender. Didn't want to hurt her with rough play.

Facing each other, their gazes took the measure of the other now that they were free from prying eyes, and the effect she had on him this close produced a clenching in his gut along with the full rise of his cock.

Her long hair rested over one petite shoulder, allowing the other curve to remain exposed under the thin strap of her nightgown. Clarke traced the scrap of silk and a shiver coursed through her.

"Are you cold?"

"No."

"Nervous?" he guessed, studying the surprisingly tranquil expression on her face. For a virgin, he expected more theatrics of fear or disgust.

Her silvery voice whispered in the scant space between them. "Yes."

"I promise to be as gentle as I can." *Or die trying.*

Iris bit her lip, the pretty pink darkening under her ministrations, and he watched in fascination, imagining following the same path with his tongue. Pulling on the tied bows topping each shoulder, drawing the silk slowly through its loop, he let the gown glide down her slight body unhindered.

And his vision of perfection was complete.

Because *she* stood before him.

Swaying from one foot to the other. Fine bones at her collar and wrists. Tender breasts tipped with blush. And the sweetest thatch of golden curls he'd ever seen gracing the juncture of her thighs.

God have mercy.

"I know I'm not much compared to other women." She gestured to her chest, embarrassment written on her features as another flush rose.

That won't do.

Clarke placed his thumb over the bitten lip and cupped her chin, the intimate hold causing Iris to tremble like a newborn colt. "You're perfect," he growled before realizing how intense it sounded in the quiet. Attempting to calm his voice and actions, he feathered a line down her neck with his fingertips and admitted in a haze of lust, "I feel like I'm in a dream. I'm lost, and you're the little sprite sent to guide me."

Such flowery words had never left his lips. But a spell of enchantment—the intoxicating presence of Iris—wove around him, and rationality fled in the wake of such magic.

"Then... follow me," she murmured in short bursts, lifting to her tiptoes and pressing her mouth to his in an artless yet utterly seductive kiss.

Aye, royally fucked.

THOUSANDS OF FIRST kisses had played out in her dreams since girlhood, but none of those figments of imagination—wisps of a summer breeze—compared to the physical exhilaration of Clarke's lips on hers. Supple and warm, they molded to her every whim until he stopped her exploratory pecks with a hand on her neck, holding her still for the swipe of his tongue.

"Let me in, little sprite."

Iris obeyed his muttered command and a gasping moan stuck in her throat at his immediate invasion. Dominant strokes of his tongue plied hers as he devoured her like a hungry beast who'd caught his prey at long last.

His mouth abandoned hers, and for a moment Iris feared he'd leave altogether—disappointed by her lack of experience—instead, Clarke trailed succulent kisses down her neck and chest until his tongue encircled a taut nipple.

"Can't hurt my sprite. Don't want to hurt you." She didn't think the words were meant for her as they were buried in her flesh, his lips pressed into her skin, but Iris responded nonetheless.

I need him to know I'm not as afraid anymore.

Somewhere between his romantic confession asserting her perfection and their kiss, Iris's fear had morphed into a much lighter emotion. One of faith and hope. Of desire.

"I trust you. You won't harm me." As if to test her resolve, he nipped at the rosebud topping her breast before suckling it with possessive force. His fingers danced upon her thigh until they reached her core and playfully tugged on the curls. Astonished by the act, Iris froze, unsure.

While Lily and Hazel had explained the basics of sex—which truthfully, she'd already discovered in a textbook of Papa's—they hadn't elaborated on specifics. They kept the details light and whimsical, sure to pique Iris's interest, ensure her lack of fear. But now she wished she hadn't been so content with their vagueness.

"You can't possibly know what I'll do. You've known me for less than a day." Clarke released her nipple long enough to chastise her blind faith before switching sides, and she didn't know how to respond. Didn't know *what* to respond to.

His words?

Or his actions?

Two fingers slid between her folds—their path eased by a startling amount of dampness—and pushed against her entrance. Instinctively recoiling at the intimate touch, the answer became clear. Now wasn't the time for a discussion.

"Dammit!" Her husband swiftly removed his hand and stepped back, leaving her cold and exposed in the eerily quiet bedroom. Confused, she tried to move closer, extending a hand out for his—desperate to fix whatever was wrong.

"Clarke...?"

"I apologize. I thought I could..." He groaned and knelt for her discarded nightgown, holding it up to her. "Here. Put this back on. That will be all for tonight."

"But... I don't understand. Did I do something wrong?" Why the sudden change?

"Wrong? This is all sorts of wrong, but it's not you." He scoffed in self-deprecation. "It's me." Striding towards the door, he opened it and checked the hallway before crossing the threshold. "I know this isn't what you envisioned for your wedding night, but I promise this is for the best for now. If you need anything, ring for one of the servants or my bedchamber is right down the hall." He pointed to the next door several yards away.

"We won't be sharing?" A silly question considering how she hadn't noticed any of his personal articles in the room, but it hadn't registered that they may not share a bed, let alone a bedroom. Her parents had. And she assumed her sisters did as well.

Iris had hoped she might avoid sleeping separately by pleasing him and praying he'd want to give their marriage a shot at success. But he'd already relegated her to another room away from him.

"No, we won't. It's not a reflection on you. I just prefer my own space." Clarke readjusted his trousers, and she noticed for the first time the impressive bulge underneath the fine fabric. *So, he desires me but refuses to take me.* "I wish you a good night."

Her echoed farewell met his back as he turned on his heel and disappeared down the hall, and her confidence before the wedding—about making him love her, of pleasing him—seemed premature after the last five minutes.

This will be more difficult than I thought.

CHAPTER SIX

"I've secured an invitation to the Taft dinner on Thursday evening. Taft has long been a friend of mine, and his wife is delighted to host my daughter's first entry into London Society." Linton preened after the announcement, clearly proud of his accomplishment, as he set aside his empty cup of tea. For Clarke's part, he supposed it was a sort of coup to have one of Society's couples accept a bastard daughter and her common husband into their esteemed home.

"How lovely! We'll be happy to attend," Iris said, an eager smile glossing over her pink lips, before she turned to Clarke, a faint cloud shadowing her eyes. "If we're free, that is. I didn't mean to assume."

Ever kind. Ever cautious.

That was his little sprite.

It amazed him how much he'd learned about her in the short time of their marriage—one week, to be exact. A time meant for honeymoons, but an event they'd skipped due to the unusual circumstances.

Probably for the best, considering how you haven't bedded her yet.

He hadn't intended on reneging on a full consummation of their marriage, but after testing the tight passage of his wife's pussy with his fingers and feeling her flinch in response, Clarke refused to burden her with the pain of his heavy cock splitting her open. No, he'd need to find another solution to deflower his virgin wife. Preferably one that didn't involve torturing Iris during her first experience of sex.

"No need to fret, sprite. If it'll make you happy, we'll go." Her beaming smile returned even brighter, causing his abdomen to ripple in something akin to butterflies at making her happy with so simple a statement.

Butterflies? Really?

The purple prose winging through his addled head these days concerned him.

Clarke didn't do romance. Didn't fall in love. And he certainly didn't do such things over a tiny ethereal woman who just so happened to be his wife.

But Iris intrigued him. Captured his thoughts with the mere whiff of her scent or sight of her belongings. Since their wedding night—an evening which painted his dreams with sex and desire, despite the small sample he'd had of her charms—he'd kept a careful distance between them. Deciding to forgo sharing a bedchamber had been a stroke of brilliance, and he'd taken to eating breakfast in his room instead of braving the dining hall where his wife could more easily heighten his obsession with her presence.

Perhaps it was cowardly. Porter would certainly find it ridiculous—a grown man avoiding the sweet sprite living in his home. But he couldn't afford to fall victim to the madness already pervading his blood.

One fragile woman claiming my love and devotion is enough.

"I'll notify Taft of your intentions to come, then." Linton smoothed a hand over his thin hair and sipped more tea from the cup resting in his hand. "You'll enjoy meeting everyone. The both of you." The older man darted a benevolent look toward Clarke as if he were bestowing a great gift upon him—entry into the upper echelons of society—and he barely managed to restrain a huff of exasperation at the notion.

"I'll write to the Dowager Countess of Trent for advice on suitable attire and proper etiquette. You won't be embarrassed by me," Iris promised. "We Hampshire girls have learned how to handle ourselves in any situation." His wife leaned closer to her father, bracing a hand on his knee for a moment before retreating, and Clarke wondered at the patience and hope she exuded.

Here was a man who'd been absent for most of her life, only to reappear with a marriage contract to a stranger years later, yet his wife held no grudges.

Only hope to please Linton and earn his approval.

"I have no doubt you'll make me proud, my dear." Linton patted her hand before standing and straightening his jacket. "Now, if you'll excuse me, I have an appointment to keep."

"Oh, I didn't realize..." Iris trailed off with a blush. "You can't stay for a second cup of tea, at least? I'd hoped we could chat more, perhaps play a game of chess like I used to with Papa... I mean, Mr. Taylor. But a game can wait for a later time."

"You may call him 'Papa' still. I don't begrudge the man the title, as he cared for you exceptionally well. And while I'd adore deepening our relationship, I'm afraid my attendance is required, or else I'd beg off." Linton's features dipped into an apologetic moue, and Clarke watched as Iris's mouth tightened, her silvery gaze dulling.

His own hands dug into the leather arms of his chair. Linton was a bastard. Despite enumerating Iris's charms to anyone who'd listen in public, the man kept himself scarce during more private meetings. This was the first time the marquess had deigned to visit them since the wedding, and he couldn't bother to linger long enough to learn about his long-lost daughter after all these years.

It annoyed Clarke. Frustrated him to no end.

Made his heart stutter pathetically at the forlorn look darkening Iris's face.

Like a lost lamb searching for its shepherd.

"I understand. Please don't fret on my account." Strained lines formed around her eyes and mouth as a grimace pretending to be a smile appeared. "We have the rest of our lives to get to know one another, so I'll work on my patience. I wish you a pleasant evening, Father." An awkward moment sprung forth as Iris's slender arms lifted to offer an embrace as Linton bent into a bow, the two of them pausing and coloring at the mismatched actions until Iris dropped into an abbreviated curtsy, forgoing the hug.

An air of rejection hung about the room, suffocating Clarke in unwanted emotions and urging him to escape. However craven the act.

"I must go as well, my dear. Previous commitment in my schedule." Nodding brusquely, he exited the room behind Linton, waving the man off as they went their separate ways—Linton to his waiting carriage and Clarke to have his horse saddled.

Tea and biscuits from earlier churned in his stomach during the entire journey to Baywater Road, and he loathed the sick feeling dogging him. *This is what I was afraid of.* He didn't want to worry about Iris. Didn't want her roiling emotions to affect his.

Yet the physical upset pummeling him at the moment attested to his failure in keeping them separate.

As a familiar terraced home came into view, Clarke begrudged the weakness when he needed to exude strength and confidence for this upcoming visit. Tying his horse to a front post, he walked the few steps to the front door and knocked before stepping inside. Quaint and quiet, soothing colors flowed down the hall to a sitting room where he found his mother, Mrs. Eliza Calloway, knitting by a fire.

"Hello, mum. How are you feeling today?" Her nurse cum companion had informed him of her high spirits shortly after receiving the letter he'd sent about marrying Iris. Apparently, she'd talked of little else since its arrival.

"Lovely, my dear. But I've missed you. Did you bring your bride? I'm longing to meet my new daughter-in-law." The elder Mrs. Calloway grinned at her son and set the tangled heap of yarn in her lap aside.

"Not today, since I wasn't sure if you'd be healthy enough for another visitor. Is Maude around? I'd like to hear how you've been doing while I've been gone."

"Maude's visiting her sister, and I'm as well as can be. See?" She raised her hands in a demonstration, tilting her head side to side as if expecting him to inspect her for falsehoods. "My heart may be weak, but you remember how spring always invigorates me with fresh energy. Along with the news of your marriage! Tell me about the girl, dear. When can I expect grandchildren?"

Sweat gathered beneath his arms, and he shrugged off his jacket before pointing to the cup and kettle by his mother's arm. "Is that lemongrass tea?" He'd discovered the plant while visiting India years ago and after learning of its beneficial properties for the heart and oral health—not to mention its calming benefits—he'd always kept a steady supply in his and his mother's homes. An exorbitant expense considering the long journey it took across the ocean, but one he was more than willing to pay if it aided his fragile mum.

And your own rushing mind.

"It is." His mother passed her cup to him with a knowing look and waited for him to take a fortifying gulp before asking again, "So... grandchildren?"

"None that I know of." He tried joking, but her stern expression sobered him quickly. "It's not quite up to me, is it? Seems a better question to ask the Lord during your prayers."

While he prayed in direct opposition of her wishes.

Hopefully, it would be a lengthy time before children, since he only planned on visiting his wife's bed sparingly—too aware of the possibility of injuring her slight form accidentally in the throes of passion. Besides, the thought of a child scared him witless. Iris's tiny body carrying a child of his? One who would no doubt be large and difficult? No, he would not force that upon her if he could help it.

"Count on it, my dear. I want grandbabies to spoil."

Clarke dipped his head in acknowledgment. "Noted. In the meantime, would you settle for a son who adores you?" He took her frail hand in his sturdier one, carefully cradling it in his palm. Since birth, his mum had suffered from shortness of breath and chronic fatigue—among other prolonged symptoms—an illness which had no cure, according to physicians. They diagnosed her with angina, recommended bottles of amyl nitrite to manage paroxysms, and went on their way without a backward glance.

Never caring how the prescription increased his mother's dizzy spells and headaches.

So, Clarke had sought different methods of relief. Lemongrass being one of them, allowing his mother to decrease usage of the amyl nitrite to its lowest doses while the herb naturally improved her daily life.

"Always. But you can never have too many people to love," she said. "Which is why I'm eager to meet your wife. Now, tell me about her and the wedding. All those high society lords and ladies!" She fluttered a hand to her chest as a dreamy sigh issued forth. "My own son living a storybook life. I couldn't have asked for anything better."

Storybook might push the bounds of reality, but he didn't correct her. She loved hearing about the exploits of the upper crust, treated them like mythical gods and goddesses meant for her entertainment and awe. And Clarke didn't care to disabuse her of the notion after learning the truth about them—how very much flesh and blood and mistakes they're made of.

"Iris was a vision in cream silk," he began and smiled fondly at the far-off gleam entering his mum's eyes as her imagination spirited away, collecting his words and weaving them into a beautiful scene of love and romance as she requested more details.

It almost made him believe there truly was magic in that day.

Almost.

CHAPTER SEVEN

A few days later, Iris found herself at the Tafts with Clarke and her father—the latter loudly singing her praises to all who were near, while the former provided off-color comments every now and again. It bordered on rude, but she couldn't help snickering at a couple of statements and everyone around them seemed to revel in the common man's uncouth point of view.

Linton's ramblings, however...

Compliments and accolades had their place, and the dinner table was not the proper locale, judging by his audience. The circle of people around him fidgeted at the flaunting of an illegitimate child, and to Iris's mind, half the traits he attributed to her weren't even true. It was as if he sought to share the perfect image of a daughter he'd built in his mind instead of the true Iris—a woman he'd yet to spend any significant time with.

And where her father had gotten the notion that Lady Taft was pleased to have his newly found daughter in her home, Iris could never guess. The lady in question refused to even glance in Iris's direction as if the words *bastard child* marked her forehead.

A respite finally came when the men and women separated to different drawing rooms after dinner—the women's decked in pinks and violets with blooms of peonies occupying the walls. Which was how Iris found herself sitting alone near a flourishing bouquet, its cloying scent agitating her nose, in a room full of society ladies who seemed to be in secret agreement to ignore her presence.

"Evelyn, what did you think of Lady Oscar's gown at the opera last night?" Lady Taft asked a woman of similar age seated to her right as a round of titters erupted from the surrounding ladies.

"Oh, that ghastly yellow one?" Lady Oscar's tall coiffure shook with the force of her head shake. "Do we know who her modiste is? Because we must take note to never darken that establishment's doorway!" Everyone agreed with sage nods or waves of their fans, and Iris felt a pang of kinship with the dismissed seamstress who'd been summarily shunned in the span of seconds.

Thank goodness Lady Trent saw to my wardrobe at Madame Fleur's.

Though it was a small consolation when her person didn't register with these women, let alone the state of her attire. *If only I had something of value to contribute.* But she doubted they'd be interested in news of the countryside, so instead, Iris wished Lily or the elder Lady Trent were here. At least then she'd have a friend. Unfortunately, both ladies remained at the Trent Estate in Hampshire while the entire family doted on baby Benjamin.

Family.

Letting the conversation swirl around her, Iris studied the intricate lines of the blooms beside her, imagining what her botanically minded adoptive parents would've seen. Mama would've painted the curling stems and varying shades of pastels coloring the petals while Papa enumerated the history of peonies and their origins.

She didn't know how Linton would react.

Probably wouldn't have noticed them...

Despite high hopes of building a deeper relationship with her father, Linton didn't seem to possess similar dreams of getting to know Iris. *Perhaps he's giving you time to adjust as a newlywed.* The charitable thought held merit, she supposed, except he'd invited Clarke and she to this dinner and spent the dinner conversing with everyone but her—talking *about* Iris instead of *with* her. He'd also declined her invitation to share a carriage ride to the Tafts, choosing to arrive on his own.

"You're quite at home with nature, aren't you, Mrs. Calloway?" A young brunette asked from her perch across the room. "The peonies are positively wreathing you in flora like a wood nymph." The ladies laughed, and Iris blushed at the comment, ashamed of being caught as a literal wallflower.

"I can't resist a pretty flower, it's true." She played along good-naturedly. "My parents—adoptive parents, that is—were quite bombastic in their love of all things botanical."

"Oh, yes. I forgot about your... irregular upbringing." Another round of giggles erupted, though this time Iris felt the edge of judgment lining their amusement. "However did you handle learning of your noble blood? Daughter of a marquess! Sounds like something out of a fairytale."

"Yes, I'll admit Cinderella came to mind when Lord Linton arrived in Shoreham to introduce himself. Thankfully, I've been friends, and more recently family, with Lord and Lady Trent my entire life, so my immediate reaction wasn't too gauche." Iris forced a polite grin, uncomfortable with the turn of discussion. She hardly knew Linton—these women even less—and sharing intimate details of such a private revelation sent an itch running over her skin.

"The Earl and Countess of Trent. I didn't realize you were close. Though that family has avoided London's festivities for years now, haven't they?"

Lady Taft stepped in with a flick of her fan. "Not since the old Earl died. Quite suddenly, I heard, but no sense in becoming hermits because of it." Her covered shoulders shrugged beneath the silk of her dress, and the discussion moved onto the appropriate amount of time for mourning husbands—as a few widows voiced their views on the subject.

Iris breathed a sigh of relief as they moved on without her, preferring the previous role of silent observer if attention only led to invasive questions regarding her family.

Cinderella, indeed.

She didn't much feel like a princess, and while she'd compared Clarke's looks to those of a fictional villain, his actual persona resembled no one so devious, nor as adoring as Prince Charming. He remained congenial. neutral in most aspects.

Their wedding night had been the one aberration with his dominant lovemaking, at least at first, before the mask of restraint fell over him, and he'd remained scarce ever since. How she wished she saw more of that dedicated lover. Or more of her husband in general.

To still be a virgin after nearly two weeks wedded.

It shamed her.

Frustrated her.

But Clarke was as elusive as a jackrabbit skipping through the forest surrounding the Trent Estate.

Avoidance seemed too strong of an adjective to describe his schedule, but with days spent separately until dinner, where stuttering conversation revolved around inane subjects, Iris wondered if Clarke *was* avoiding her. Why, though?

You heard him say he didn't want to marry you at the church.

The recalled conversation played in her mind again, and she remembered the resolve she felt to prove her strength to Clarke—to prove his assessment of her frailty wrong. But how to do such a thing when he was about as present in her life as Linton?

A course of action failed to materialize upon reflection, and Iris lamented her current predicament. *If only I could ask for help...* But sharing a marital problem with her sisters so soon after the wedding didn't sit well. Any favor Clarke found with her family at the reception would be demolished, and she couldn't stomach that consequence when all she wanted was harmony between everyone.

But they couldn't continue in their current vein.

She loathed sleeping apart from him, trusting that closer quarters would hasten their bonding. And while it was sweet that he took his responsibility of protecting her seriously, she'd hardly melt under the rain like he'd assumed on their way to the dinner—cursing Jimmy and himself for forgetting an umbrella. As if Iris had never been caught in a storm before.

He needed to see that she was made of sturdier stock than her physical appearance would have one believe.

"Mrs. Calloway, perhaps you can answer Miss Tabetha's question." Beckoned back into the fray of gossiping women, Iris nodded, praying the query would be repeated since she'd drifted too far into her own thoughts to pay attention to those around her. "Do roses naturally bloom blue?"

Furrow lines formed between Iris's brows as she considered the odd question. "Blue, my lady?"

"Yes, I saw them with my maid as we traversed Bond Street. These ladies, however, don't believe me. They think I misidentified the flower." Miss Tabetha huffed. "As if I can't discern a rose from a petunia."

"Well..." Iris cleared her throat, searching the years spent in a family of botanists for an answer. "I don't believe roses occur naturally in that color, but it's possible to dye flowers. Perhaps that's what you saw."

The young woman smirked in smug satisfaction while some of the older women harrumphed at being corrected. "I knew they were roses! Thank you, Mrs. Calloway, for your input. It seems a life raised in the country has its uses, after all."

And just like that, the order of things restored itself, with Iris promptly reminded of her lower place in their circle. *How much longer must I endure this?* A wilting peony drooped near her shoulder, and she surreptitiously broke it off from the stem, pulling its petals off and piling them in her lap—a fragrant, desolate composition of pink.

There's a metaphor in here, I'm sure.

Something about pretty objects and their fragility, but she would not so easily fall victim to cliché.

CHAPTER EIGHT

*M*um *will enjoy the story of tonight. Nobles gowned in silks dining on caviar and champagne.*

The errant thought floated through Clarke's tired mind as he emptied his nightcap before heading upstairs to his room. Exhaustion settled on his shoulders, and he rubbed his neck to loosen some of the tension built from an evening of holding his tongue and pretending civility with Linton.

The man had no shame, and the Taft dinner proved it. Jabbering on about Iris as if she were a product of his superior parenting skills and not the loving upbringing she received from her aunt and uncle.

Clarke's teeth clenched at the hours he'd had to endure with the lord and his cronies—the one silver lining was Iris escaping the uncomfortable discourse after dinner. Because if he'd witnessed another wince of her nose or paling of her cheeks due to Linton, the evening might have ended altogether differently.

I wonder what my little sprite is up to now...

He wanted to go to Iris. Knock on her door to assure himself of her well-being.

But such an act edged too close to admitting feelings that had no place in his life.

Nearly two weeks of your marriage down, only the rest of your life to go.

The prospect of remaining at a safe distance for so long daunted him, but this fascination of his would surely cool with time. Everything was still new and unexpected. Once Iris's presence in his life dulled to the monogamy of marriage, his task wouldn't be so difficult.

She'd be deeply ensconced in his protection, and his concern over her fragility would fade to a manageable level.

Light streamed through an open doorway as he passed the library, and a prickling in his gut urged him to enter. *It's probably nothing*, he reasoned. Yet Clarke never ignored those premonitions—a trait he must've inherited from his mother with her love of magical tales—because it was the rare superstition he allowed himself.

Wavering outside the entry, his gaze studied the dim room until it landed on a figure curled in the window seat, white cotton draped over slender shoulders and legs to brush the floor where one foot swung back and forth. A lilting melody hummed in the air—morose and haunting—a reflection of its singer's emotions.

This is dangerous.

But he couldn't abandon Iris when she looked so forlorn. Knee drawn to her chest with arms wrapped protectively around it. An air of melancholy encompassing her.

Berating himself, Clarke cautiously stepped inside the library, his booted feet muted by a thick Persian rug. "Didn't expect to find you here. Couldn't sleep after tonight's festivities?" he ventured, sticking to the shadows surrounding the one beam of moonlight.

Iris remained quiet. The minute tightening around her shoulders and the ceasing of her humming were the only indicators that she'd heard him.

"Couldn't stop my thoughts from running wild..." she finally said without glancing at him. Then lower, added almost as an afterthought, "I didn't fit in."

"A positive thing, to be sure." Clarke neared her hunched position, luminescent light gilding her in an ethereal glow like she truly was the little sprite he'd named her. "You're kinder, prettier, and altogether more interesting than those old matrons."

Iris darted an exasperated look his way. "I appreciate the sentiment, but I meant that they understand each other, and my father's world, better than I ever will, and it showed tonight. The only thing of interest about me was my odd lineage—the one topic I didn't want to discuss."

"You mean you don't prefer being known as the illegitimate offspring of Lord Linton?"

Joke falling flat, Iris's melancholic expression stuck firmly in place. Clarke kneeled beside her and followed her view out to the small courtyard at the rear of their home. "Sorry for the poor attempt at humor. I understand why your father would be a sore subject."

"Do you?" Piercing silver shot his way. "Because no one else seems to, least of all Linton himself. My family presses and prods for more information. Individual letters from Cara, Hazel, Lily, and Owen. Each trying in their own way to warn me away from getting too close to my father, while at the same time wishing me the best in my endeavors. In the meantime, Linton has hardly spent an hour in my presence and acts like everything's settled between us. Spouting my praises to everyone he meets. The ever-loving father and his long-lost daughter."

Iris's chest heaved with a deep breath before continuing, her small hands clenched in the folds of her nightgown. "Don't mistake me. I want our relationship to reach that point. But how can it when he evades my every effort at connection? I thought..." Her voice broke for a moment before recovering, and Clarke's heart squeezed at the obvious effort being made. Marveled at the deluge of words raining down upon him. His shy wife stuttered and stalled around him usually, yet her nerves appeared overcome by frustration, pain. "I thought my agreement to this marriage scheme of his—no offense intended—would cement a firmer foundation beneath us. Would garner some sort of affection or interest in knowing me better. Why does he still deflect every attempt I make to deepen our relationship?"

The true cause of her distress revealed, his little sprite rested her head on the windowpane in despair, tiny puffs of heat fogging the glass. If Linton were present, he would've found himself quickly thrown to the ground by a swift punch to the gut because Clarke hated seeing Iris so wounded. Especially when it stemmed from a narcissistic gambler who only cared to use Iris for what he could gain financially—not a familial relationship.

"I'm not sure he's consciously evading you out of spite. Your father didn't grow up in a quaint village in the country like you. Didn't live in close quarters with multiple siblings and loving parents. It's not how most children are raised in his world. If we're being honest, he's treating you the way most men treat their daughters in society: marrying her off for his own benefit." Clarke shrugged broad shoulders and clasped a hand around her knee. "It's not a very flattering tradition, and I apologize for becoming a key part in the plan, but there you have it."

"I don't blame you for anything. Out of everyone, you're the only person who hasn't pushed me one way or the other about my father." She paused before a speculative gleam entered her silver eyes. "Why did you agree to his proposition?"

Clarke froze under her gentle but inquisitive gaze. None of his original reasons sounded good enough now. In fact, they sounded downright despicable in light of his wife's presence. The way he'd planned to use her. The sick satisfaction of sticking it to the upper crust, a class she really didn't belong to either.

He considered lying, prettying up a tale of hope for the future, full of romantic rot she'd love, but the words wouldn't come. Honesty won out. "I wanted to nab myself a lady, no matter your illegitimacy, to rub it in Society's face—a lady wed to the son of a sailor and butcher's daughter. A flimsy and ridiculous reason to chain us together for life, I see that now, but it is what it is."

"I'm surprised you valued Society's comeuppance at so high a price. Five thousand pounds for bragging rights." An incredulous giggle gushed forth as Iris tried to hide it behind the palm of her hand. "I'm sorry, but you're quite right. It's extremely foolish."

Clarke nodded in assent, a wry smile lifting the corners of his mouth. "What can I say except I have money to spare, and I probably would've married eventually, just to keep my mum happy. Didn't seem like too much of a leap to pay for a lady instead of settling for some other chit."

"It wouldn't be settling if you were in love." Iris pointed out, and a hazy film ghosted over her eyes. As if she felt sorry for him. As if she regretted being the reason he'd never find love.

"Don't concern yourself over that far-fetched possibility. I never planned on marrying for love."

"Why not? Because of your parents?"

He shook his head and lowered into a more comfortable position on the floor beside her, his shoulder resting against the opposite end of the window seat as he looked up at Iris. His hand caught her swinging foot and brought it to rest on his leg, unconsciously massaging the delicate bones and tendons before replying. "No, they were madly in love. Like one of those books my mum adores, my father saw her on the street and knew she was the one. Proposed a week later."

"A love match!" Iris perked up at the information, and her enthusiasm came as no surprise. He'd caught sight of some of the books she toted around—romance and fairytales, the lot of them. "How romantic! Yet you didn't want to emulate their marriage in your own?"

"Never felt the desire, no."

"I suppose it makes sense in a roundabout way..." Iris mused, leaning forward to rest her chin on an upraised knee, and he admired the fall of wavy hair as it slid down her arm in slow motion until the ends tickled his skin. "Marriage isn't as necessary for men's survival as it is for women. We have little else offered to us."

The sentiment echoed his original thoughts after hearing Linton's proposition at the club weeks ago. "A failing in our society, to be sure." Companionable silence twined between them, wispy filaments threading together to form a stronger bond. It didn't bind and choke—forcing compliance—rather, it coaxed and teased, urging one to give in to its promise of serenity.

And the intimate temptation slammed Clarke back to reality. *I need to redirect this to familiar territory.* A dangerous place, in its own right, but for an entirely different reason.

Sliding a hand under her nightgown, he caressed a shapely calf before trailing higher and brushing a thumb across the delicate skin behind her knee.

Iris kept her eyes on him, curiosity mingling with bewilderment. "What are you doing?"

"Isn't it obvious?" He gently lifted her leg to rest over his shoulder while his other side rested against the window seat—giving him the perfect opportunity to kiss her inner thigh.

"The obvious answer would be that we're about to make love, but since you've avoided me for weeks now, I'm not sure I trust my judgment."

Then we're two peas in a pod.

Because Clarke wasn't sure he could trust his, either.

Rubbing his cheek along her silky skin, he fought for a semblance of control—tried to focus on how to please her safely instead of worrying about what could go wrong. "It's not that I dislike your company. It's that I like it *too* much," he admitted. "And a craving like mine is difficult to handle at the best of times—being near you... Well, let's just say I lacked conviction in my restraint."

"But now you don't."

A cynical chuckle emerged at her statement. "No, I still highly doubt this is a good idea. You bruise too easily under my fingertips. But I hate seeing you brought so low, and I'm tired of denying myself the pleasure of your body. We'll learn together if I've made the right decision."

Iris stroked his cheek and offered a reassuring smile. "You have. It is. I've longed for this moment. I've just been too uncertain—too timid—to voice my desire."

"Oh, little sprite. You never need to worry about telling me what you need. I only wish to keep you safe and happy. Whatever you want is yours." Perhaps he should've made that clearer early on instead of evading run-ins with his wife.

His eyes devoured the pretty picture she made, gilded in moonlight and shadows, her night rail playing a rousing game of hide and seek with the pink buds of her nipples. More enticing than any naked woman he'd seen at Martin's, where mystery didn't exist.

One of these days, he'd have Iris tease her breasts while he ate her cunt. Those nimble fingers toying with the sensitive flesh, reddening taut... *Enough!* Clarke's thready control shook with the force of will it took to erase the beguiling image. He couldn't afford any more temptation—inhaling Iris's scent of arousal was more than sufficient.

"Close your eyes and relax," Clarke growled, unable to muster a calmer tone. "You don't have to concern yourself with a single thing. Your husband will take care of everything."

Waiting until Iris obeyed, he set himself to the delightful task of pursuing the faint path of veins along her thigh once her lashes fluttered shut. Gentle licks of his tongue traced and dipped, showering each leg with equal attention before reaching his goal—her sweet pussy, perfectly framed by the crumpled hem of her nightgown. The blonde curls beckoned, urging him to search their depths for the treasure they protected.

Fingers contracting around Iris's hips, Clarke dove forward like a hawk sighting its prey and nuzzled the hidden flesh until his nose brushed her clitoris, his tongue burrowing within her sleek walls. A hitch in her breath sounded from above, and his wife's hands clutched his shoulders for support.

"Clarke... What..."

"Shhh... It's just a kiss, little sprite. Isn't this what you wanted?" He intimated their last kiss, his tongue plunging deep before retreating, laving the glistening bud topping her sex with lavish strokes. "Don't you want my kisses? Your body's primed for them. Slick and swollen with need. My pretty little wife hungry for her husband's touch."

A moan of agreement vibrated down Iris's rocking form, her hips fighting his grip to press deeper into his mouth, and he happily obliged. Charmed by her brazen insistence, Clarke devoted himself to indulging in the delectable treat that was his wife. She hummed, then gasped—nails biting into his shoulders—as he worked her body into a frenzy of lust, licking and sucking every sweet part of her he could reach until a resounding cry filled the library.

An echoing spurt of seed dampened his trousers in response, his aching cock desperate for a similar release.

Dropping a hand to squeeze the thick flesh into submission, Clarke focused on easing Iris through her climax, gentling his tongue before finally edging away once she began pushing at him.

"That... was... wonderful." Iris sighed, and he lowered her legs off his shoulders to the floor. "And you... enjoyed it?"

"Very much so," he grunted. His gaze studied the heightened color on her cheeks then dropped to the points of her breasts, almost pitching forward to steal a sample of their berried fruit, before faint marks on Iris's legs caught his attention.

Bruises.

From him.

He'd been too rough.

She didn't seem to mind.

But Clarke did. Iris was fragile even if she'd deny it, and he loathed seeing the evidence of his coarseness on her skin. Hell, if he couldn't be trusted to treat her tenderly during an experiment of his control, how could he bring himself to fuck her like he wanted to? To consummate their damn marriage?

The answer was he couldn't.

Not yet.

"Shall we head upstairs?" Iris shyly asked, oblivious to his inner turmoil. "I could..." She sought the bulge in his trousers, her intentions clear, and Clarke jumped to his feet, backing away from her generous offer.

Christ, if she held his cock in those innocent hands, he may actually die from ecstasy.

"Yes, I think we both need our rest." He shuffled backward. "I'll see you tomorrow. Good night." With a stilted bow,

Clarke escaped to his bedchambers, where he swiftly locked the door and ripped his clothes off, choking his cock in a firm grip.

Bracing a hand on the bedpost, he stroked himself and closed his eyes to picture Iris as she looked downstairs. Flushed face. Bright eyes. Arousal evident on every inch of her skin. And her taste! It lingered in his mouth, urged him to pull roughly at his cock and spread slick pre-cum along its hard length as Clarke imagined the bulging tip resting on his wife's tongue. Pictured painting her pretty pink lips with his seed.

Groaning at the lewd vision, his stones drew up before a few jerky strokes of his coarse palm caused Clarke to spend on to the bedspread before him.

Instead of his little sprite like he dreamed.

A dream that could've been a reality, if he hadn't run away. *Fucking coward.*

CHAPTER NINE

He gave her gifts instead of orgasms.

After their intimate interlude in the library, Clarke didn't avoid her as often, even choosing to finally dine with her during breakfast, but he still kept his own chambers, never frequenting her bed. She'd hoped the passion shared would be a breakthrough in their relationship. Thought it would raise her husband's estimation of her strength and durability, but they hadn't made love since the evening of the Taft dinner.

Instead, he gave her gifts.

Beautiful, expensive *gifts*.

Which she appreciated and accepted with gratitude, but Iris would rather have her husband than another set of earrings.

And not just for naughty purposes.

With Clarke gone during the day and staff to handle the majority of the housework, Iris struggled to keep herself occupied. Boredom had never been a problem for her in the past, since three sisters kept things lively at home. But in London, she had no one.

Finished embroidering Clarke's initials to the last of his shirt cuffs—a small gesture to show her care and hopefully add to her worthiness as a wife—she collected the stack of clothing to drop off in her husband's room and wondered at what to do next.

"I need to make myself *useful*." Determined, Iris headed downstairs to chat with Mrs. Franklin—perhaps she could help with a chore of some kind. She found the woman sitting in the kitchen speaking with Mrs. Marks while helping her peel potatoes.

"Good afternoon, ladies. May I help with anything? I'm happy to pitch in," Iris offered and immediately saw her mistake as both women exchanged looks of horror at the lady of the house offering to do manual labor.

"Oh, no, that won't be necessary." Mrs. Franklin recovered first. "Why don't you have Jimmy show you around town? Go shopping? You haven't explored London yet, have you?"

"Not really..."

"Well, what are you waiting for, dear?" Both women smiled encouragingly, and Iris couldn't help but reluctantly agree to their suggestion. She didn't want to make them uncomfortable, after all.

"You're right. It's high time I learned more about my new home," she said, effecting an air of excitement despite her inner lack of enthusiasm. Part of the joy of exploring was in the company one kept, yet she'd be traipsing through London alone save for the coachman.

Gathering her gloves and hat, Iris waited for Mrs. Franklin to notify Jimmy of their impending trip and contemplated where to go. She didn't need any more jewelry—Clarke took care of that. Her armoire was already overflowing with day dresses and party gowns, so a visit to the modiste wasn't necessary.

What to do, what to do...

Fiddling with the wedding ring on her finger, the obvious answer lurched forward in a flash. So, when Jimmy sat at attention atop the carriage a quarter of an hour later, instead of announcing Bond Street, she directed him to Linton Place—the home of her father.

She'd never visited him at the family residence, but surely, he wouldn't begrudge her impulsive decision to call without notice. A vision of his pleased expression formed in her mind, graying hair mussed from a quick run-through of his hand to make himself presentable, smile lines creasing his eyes and mouth.

Perhaps catching him unawares, showing him the depth of her commitment to an enduring relationship between them, would be the catalyst to achieving everything she'd hoped for once learning of his existence.

Upon their arrival at Linton Place, however, a baffled sort of shock ran down her spine. "Are you sure this is it?" she asked Jimmy as he helped her down to the sidewalk.

"Yes, ma'am. The original Linton home was in Kensington, but a year ago, Lord Linton moved the household to this terraced house."

"I see..." Except she didn't. Because this home was nothing like she expected. Years ago, on a visit to their father in London, the Taylors drove down the affluent neighborhoods of the elite, exclaiming over the gleaming marble columns and trimmed foliage. It was no secret that Society's lords and ladies occupied extravagant abodes.

Yet Iris's father—a marquess—had left the shining jewel of London for... this?

While not quite in shambles, the slightly sagging roof and chipped brick spoke of difficult times, and for the first time, she truly wondered what exactly happened for her father to require five thousand pounds from Clarke or else face violence. Because a person didn't choose to step down from their rightful place in Society—from their family's legacy—unless they encountered serious financial trouble.

Perhaps she should've questioned him more about the circumstances earlier, but a part of her just wanted to bask in the hope of a budding relationship with her father, without the pall of his flaws coloring her opinion of him. Eventually, those things would appear—as would hers—but Iris wanted to live in a bubble of hope and potential for as long as possible.

It would seem my bubble, however, is about to burst.

Gnawing on her bottom lip, Iris slowly traversed the entryway, observing more signs of neglect, before tapping a brass knocker against the door. An older woman with faded red hair answered the summons.

"Yes?"

The barked question startled her with its hostility. *Surely, this can't be right.* "Hello, I'm Mrs. Iris Calloway, Lord Linton's daughter. I thought I might visit him if he's available, but I'm not sure—"

"Is he expecting you?"

"No, and I realize it's unbearably rude to call uninvited, but I—"

The woman cut her off again. "Don't get many *invited* guests either. You said you're his daughter? The bastard?" Her left eye squinted as if searching for a resemblance before giving up and waving Iris inside with an impatient hand.

"He's in there. Enjoy your visit." A harsh cackle erupted from this strange... housekeeper? Maid? Iris wasn't quite certain how to identify her but followed a pointing finger towards a closed room to her right.

"Um... Thank you. I appreciate your assistance." Removing the emerald hat from her head, Iris tried the doorknob and carefully pushed it forward. "Hello? Father? It's me, Iris, are you in here?"

Dim light blanketed the room, dust motes floating in the air and tickling her nose until an uncontrollable sneeze burst forth. A delayed *bless you* rose from a chaise along the wall in the darkest part of the room.

"Father? Are you ill?"

"Iris... darling? What are... you doing... here?" Long pauses fell between each belabored word as Linton struggled to a sitting position—not even attempting to rise at her entry. Reaching for a braided rope near the window, Iris pulled the drapes open to let in more light and was stunned at Linton's disheveled appearance.

His stained collar lay open across his chest while a wrinkled jacket hung haphazardly from his shoulders, but the most obvious sign of trouble came from bleary, bloodshot eyes, which Linton quickly covered once the addition of extra sunlight reached him.

"What happened? Were you awake all night?" Iris hurried to his side and joined him on the chaise, an ominous creak emitting from the furniture at her slight weight.

"Unfortunately." Linton scrubbed slim fingers over his eyes while a waft of alcohol surrounded him, battling the dust in the air for the most offensive item to Iris's senses.

She'd never witnessed the aftereffects of an inebriated man—never witnessed a man so deep in his cups, to be honest. The fact that her first experience with such a dismal sight was due to her father's overindulgence made it all the more disappointing.

So much for surprising him, Iris thought ruefully. For he'd thoroughly shocked her instead.

"Let me fetch some tea. Perhaps it will restore you to better spirits." Offering a soothing refreshment seemed the one task she could do to help him, since this was so far out of the realm of her knowledge. Leaving him to marinate on the chaise, Iris left the room and followed the hall towards the back of the home, praying she'd find the kitchen empty of Linton's brusque staff member.

Dirty dishes piled high on the counter as her search ended in a small offshoot from the hall, pots and pans hung from a fixture in the ceiling, and fruit flies flitted about. *Scratch housekeeper off the list.* Because what self-respecting housekeeper would leave the kitchen in such disarray?

Iris clucked her tongue in disapproval and maneuvered around the cramped space to find a kettle and teacups resting in a cupboard, a fine layer of dust dulling the floral patterns painted on the sides. *This won't do.* No stranger to hard work, the promise of an afternoon spent cleaning and organizing didn't faze her—in fact, it comforted her with its familiarity.

Gloves removed and sleeves unbuttoned so she could roll them to her elbows, Iris cleared a working area and washed the kettle and cups first to start Linton's tea. Once a kettle of water was placed on the stove, the monumental task of sorting through used plates, silverware, and various cooking utensils commenced. At one point—between Iris delivering hot tea to Linton and her scrubbing a particularly stubborn casserole dish—the mysterious servant poked her head into the kitchen to see what the bustle was about before disappearing, a gruff "Olga" emitted when asked her name.

Several hours passed without a word from anyone, Olga and Linton apparently content with sticking to their respective rooms in the home. Iris scoured the counters and floor, polished a mountain of silverware, and prepared a meal for her father when he was ready to consume something more substantial than tea. It felt good to be needed, even if the circumstances weren't ideal.

I think you mean downright abysmal.
But we're moving in the right direction.

Soon, she'd have her father's house sorted, even if she had to complete every task herself. Declaring an end to the chores for the time being, Iris checked on Linton one last time before leaving. "I'm about to go home, Father. I left supper for you in the kitchen. Is there anything else I can get you before I go?"

Linton pushed to his feet, marginally more stable than he was earlier, and toddled over to her.

"There is one thing... But I hate to ask when you've been so good to me..."

Enfolding his hand in hers, she massaged the wrinkled and spotted skin. "Nonsense. I'm your daughter. I want to help you however I can."

Linton's thin lips lifted in a grateful smile. "Thank you, my dear. You're a good girl." He squeezed her palm. "Unfortunately, I'm in a bit of a bind with Olga—the woman who let you in. You see, with the chaos of your wedding and those threatening men, I've gotten behind on her wages."

That would explain the lack of work being done.

"A loan would be much appreciated, if you're able. Olga's been with the Linton household for years, and I hate for her to suffer because of me." His rheumy eyes pleaded with her, and Iris was helpless to deny him.

"Of course, though I'm afraid I don't carry much coin... But I could transfer funds from my personal account at the bank. Owen... I mean, the Earl of Trent and Clarke have both been kind enough to ensure I have whatever I need for shopping and the like. How much do you need?"

"I'm afraid a transfer will take too long. Olga takes care of her sister's family as well as her own, and if I can't pay her quickly... Well, I hate to think what might befall her poor family. Her sister's bedridden, you know?" A flash of sympathy appeared in his eyes before Linton tapped the clasped band of her bracelet with a knowledgeable wink. "What about this bracelet? Diamonds, is it? Pearls are much more your style, dear, so you could think of it as a relief to part with it."

"My bracelet?" It was her first purchase in London as a married woman. A sort of gift to commemorate so much change in her life.

An extravagant and unnecessary one.

Is it right to let a poor woman stay penniless? Let her family suffer and allow Father to live in filth because of it?

No.

She couldn't allow that to happen when she was fortunate enough to be able to stop it.

Unsnapping the bracelet from her wrist, the glittering strand swung between them before Linton snatched it from her hand. "Thank you, dear. I know a man who will pay an excellent price for this trinket. You have no idea how much this means to me. And Olga, of course." Slipping past her, he opened the front door with exaggerated fanfare. "Let me wish you a safe journey home, and please tell your husband how glad I am to see you looking so well."

The abrupt transition from distressed to jovial was remarkable. One would almost never know that her father had been three sheets to the wind mere hours earlier, except for the stench emanating from him. Suspicion hovered at the edges of her mind, but she dismissed it.

So, he was happy. Why shouldn't he be? Olga will now be able to perform her duties properly, and he'll enjoy a well-kept home. There's no reason to doubt his motive or intention for the money.

Linton stood in the entryway, some of his pep dissolving. "Is everything alright? I see your coachman waiting—you won't have to dally about the sidewalk for his arrival."

Ignoring the inkling of doubt at the back of her mind, Iris offered a strained smile before heading outside. "Everything's quite fine. I will see you again soon, Father." She dropped a quick peck to his cheek and let Jimmy help her into the carriage, sinking into a velvet seat with a hand to her abdomen.

Stop fretting. You did the right thing.

Rubbing soothing circles over the heavy pit in her stomach, she prayed, "I certainly hope so."

CHAPTER TEN

A ruffled Iris with hair askew and reddened hands arrived home at the same time as Clarke, and immediately his guard went up. "Where have you been? Are you alright?" His normally calm and groomed wife resembled a harried washerwoman with tendrils of blonde escaping her coiffure, her previously impeccable gown wrinkled and stained in places. And was that lye he smelled?

Once inside their foyer, he impulsively grabbed her hands, gently caressing the abused skin as she haltingly explained. "I visited my father today. His household has fallen into disarray, so I decided to set it back to rights."

"You spent the day cleaning Linton's home as if you were his damn housemaid?" In retrospect, perhaps his tone could've been less forceful—more concerned—but the image of Iris on her knees scrubbing a grubby floor, wearing herself thin for a man who couldn't care less about her well-being, burned a hole in his gut. Forcing a measure of calm, he added, "You could've overworked yourself. Been injured."

Iris laughed, brows drawing up in bafflement. "From tidying a home? Clarke, don't forget I spent most of my life completing household chores without the aid of servants."

"And don't forget you're *my* wife now." Another deep breath. "You're not required to do such things anymore. If

Linton can't see to his own household staff, then I'll deal with it because you shouldn't have to."

"I can't let you do that." A stricken expression tightened the lines around her mouth and eyes. "He's my father, and you've already helped so much. I have my trust from Owen, along with the dowry he settled upon me, which you refused. I'll sort out any hiring that's needed and make sure he's cared for."

The idea of her using another man's money...

"Absolutely not. As your husband, it's my duty to care for you, which extends to your family—including Linton."

An adorable growl of frustration emanated from her, and he realized they were having their first argument. In truth, he'd wondered if his little sprite even felt such base emotions like anger and frustration with the way she exuded serenity in every situation he'd seen her tossed in.

Absent father?

Snobby Society women?

Handled like a true lady with class.

But dare to challenge her view of right and wrong, and it seemed her calm flew out the window. It was an endearingly human quality.

Choosing to offer a compromise, Clarke added, "If you must insert yourself into Linton's troubles, then I suppose you may work on staffing his home with help from Mrs. Franklin and with *my* money. Agreed?"

She chewed her bottom lip, mulling over his words. "Agreed. Though I don't want to burden Mrs. Franklin with more work when she's already searching for people to staff our home as it is."

"We'll see what she says when asked." He didn't want to overburden the women either, but Iris would need help hiring and managing two household staffs for the time being. Mind racing from one problem-solving idea to the next, a possible fix to all their problems materialized as he considered his own connections with the world of hospitality. "It just occurred to me that I may have a solution to our staffing problems in both houses. Why don't I speak with Porter about our current roster of hotel employees? We may be able to recommend those who are looking for a different environment from the Grand Markham."

"I think it's an excellent idea to consult with him. Together, our homes will be righted in no time." Iris's face lit up with a smile, and she reached out to squeeze his forearm in appreciation. A zing shot straight through his arm and into his heart before jetting lower to his cock. Pride like he'd never felt before swelled to Napoleonic proportions, and an overwhelming urge to kiss her pulsed forward.

A kiss would be appropriate, he reasoned. They'd fought; they'd made up. A friendly kiss would only cement the restored order of things.

You don't do friendly.

But he hadn't had a wife before. Husbands kissed their wives after an argument. He was sure of it.

"Thank you, sprite. Shall we kiss on it?"

Lashes fluttered and eyebrows rose infinitesimally. But it was her mouth he focused on. Lips parting to allow her pink tongue to swipe against the delicate flesh, leaving an alluring shine that beckoned him nearer.

"Kiss on it?"

Clarke crowded into her, urging Iris back into the foyer wall. Any one of their five servants could round the corner or descend the stairs, yet he didn't give a damn. Since their evening in the library, he'd wracked his brain for a way forward in their relationship and a decision had formed in his mind, a way to live with his beguiling wife while holding himself in check. And kisses were the answer.

Kisses everywhere.

And no touching by her.

Circling Iris's slim wrists, he pressed them to the wall at her sides, ensuring she couldn't tempt him with sweet caresses. His plan could only work without her interference.

"I believe it's a natural conclusion to marital spats—an embrace of reconciliation." Spicy floral notes intoxicated him as he leaned down to brush her mouth with his. She wore the perfume he'd had made for her specifically. A combination of her namesake irises, along with cardamom, cedar, and pink pepper. Apparently, irises contained a subtle scent, a trait that didn't surprise Clarke in the least after discovering his wife's quiet personality, and needed to be paired with strong woodsy aromas to create the perfect combination.

He'd listened politely to the perfumer as the man explained the intricacies of building a signature fragrance, and now gratitude filled Clarke at the proof of his expertise because Iris smelled delicious.

Good enough to eat.

No. The internal reprimand bellowed in his mind. A friendly kiss. That's what he'd give her instead of a tongue-fucking.

Dammit.

Don't think about...

His spiraling thoughts halted in the wake of a low moan purring in Iris's throat. Pressing his advantage, Clarke peppered kisses across her lips before flicking the seam of her mouth—asking for permission to enter. And being the good little wife Iris was, she complied immediately, giving him access to her honey flavor.

It really was unfair how utterly delectable she tasted, and how utterly unable he was to lose himself in her.

Because he must retain control of his desires, couldn't let them fly off the handle to potentially harm her.

But you can't live like a damn monk for the rest of your life.

No, he couldn't. Even now, with her arms pinned to the wall, Iris's slight curves swayed against his tense muscles, threatening to shatter his resolve in a public hallway.

"Free me," she begged. "I want to touch you."

"That's too dangerous, sprite. I'm afraid I already may be bruising your wrists in this hold. No telling what marks I'll leave behind if you touch me, rousing my lust to a fever pitch."

"I don't care. I trust you." Iris pressed harder into him, attempting to tug her hands out of his grip, but she was a bunny fighting the hunter's snare. She wouldn't be free until he released her. Proving his greater strength, Clarke allowed more of his weight to fall into the cushion of her slight body, subduing her movements.

"You should care. You should be wary," he warned. "You barely reach my shoulder, sprite. I'd bet my thigh is as thick as your tiny waist. I could hurt you with the smallest snap of my control, and it wouldn't be on purpose—*never on purpose*—but we would regret it all the same. That's why we must do this my way, even if it means keeping those delicate hands at your side instead of around my cock."

"But..."

"No, Iris." Silencing her protest with one final kiss, Clarke stepped back from the precipice and admired his handiwork—the dusky pink of her lips darkened, her silver eyes a swirling pool of mercury. Clearing his throat, he swiped a hand across the skin of his overheated cheeks and forced a cheery tone as if they hadn't just walked a fine ledge. "Now that we've kissed and made up. Shall we adjourn to our chambers to change for dinner? I must confess I'm starving." *For more than food, but I'll take what I can get.*

"Umm... yes, let's. I find I'm quite ravenous as well."

Surely, she didn't mean for that to sound as seductive as it did. Not his innocent little wife. But a tentative grin winked up at him, and his heart and cock jerked at her bold innuendo. *No... monkhood is not for me.* Determined to find a solution sooner rather than later, Clarke stifled a chuckle as they ascended the staircase—his boundaries extending again.

All because of one little sprite.

He was considering the possibility of tying her to a bedpost upstairs to continue their interlude—*surely, keeping her hands bound from straying too close will prevent her from completely demolishing my restraint*—when a frazzled Jones appeared at the bottom of the stairs, his clothing speckled with dirt.

"I apologize for the intrusion, but there's been an incident outside with Jimmy. Unfortunately, he fell off a ladder while attempting to repair a loose shutter. He's conscious and not seriously injured as far as I can tell. However, I think it best if we call for a doctor." Jones ran a shaky hand through his hair and stared wide-eyed up at them.

Reversing his trajectory, Clarke headed back downstairs and nodded in agreement. "Of course. Please send for someone immediately while I check on Jimmy to see for myself how he's doing."

"And I'll join you," Iris added, concern replacing her previous desire. Her hand found his as they reached the foyer again, and he couldn't help the thrill of delight the simple gesture caused him.

If they couldn't have a stolen moment abed—something that was probably for the best, considering his state of control anyway—holding hands with his wife wasn't a terrible replacement.

Careful... This reeks of sentimentality and emotions best left lukewarm.

Unfortunately, he was afraid the path to *lukewarm* was bypassed long before he even had a choice in the matter. It seemed from the moment he'd met Iris that his feelings leaned more towards the fiery end of the spectrum, despite his best efforts to curb the flames. The issue now was to learn how to shape such an extreme into something less harmful to his little sprite, something that would warm rather than burn.

Not a difficult task at all, he thought sardonically before setting the conundrum aside to focus on his injured coachman. *See to Jimmy's health first, then your responsibility as a husband.*

Perhaps tomorrow at the office Clarke could set aside a time to create a plan of action. He'd waffled between avoiding the topic or thinking about it in short spurts before the task overwhelmed him with its apparent futility for weeks now.

Maybe dedicating a concentrated effort towards solving the problem was the answer.

Can't hurt to try.

"LINTON WAS AT JACKSON'S yesterday." Porter casually tossed the information out the next morning as Clarke signed documents approving the groundbreaking of a new hotel site in Bath. They sat in his office at their first venture into the hospitality business: the Grand Markham Hotel.

At six stories tall, the Grand Markham offered posh accommodation to an array of wealthy clientèle who chose to visit London for business or pleasure. Glittering with Corinthian columns, white marble floors and rich sandalwood furniture provided visitors with a level of luxury which never failed to surprise guests.

One of Clarke's gut feelings could be thanked for his part in the hotel's success. He'd met Porter at Martin's, the two men bonding over a common background of sailors for fathers whilst a game of faro continued around them. Boisterous and witty, Porter matched Clarke in charm, and they enjoyed evenings about town gambling and womanizing before deciding to partner in a joint business deal.

"Should that surprise me? The man has a terrible habit of losing his money, and Jackson's is the perfect place to do it." Despite needing Iris's help to run his household due to financial constraints, Linton hadn't learned his lesson about playing too deep.

As if selling your only daughter wouldn't be lesson enough.

Clarke's fingers clenched on the stopper he was using to refill his fountain pen's ink reservoir, and black ink squirted over the sheet of numbers swimming before him. "Dammit!" Tugging a handkerchief from his pocket, his other hand knocked into the main inkwell and sent it tumbling over as well, black dye staining the parchment with no hope of being stopped—this page of hotel figures lay ruined.

"Surprise you? Maybe not, but it's clearly upset you." Porter rang for a maid who promptly took over cleaning the mess of ink and paper spreading to the desk underneath. "I thought you warned him against racking up debts again."

"I did. In no uncertain terms." Clarke recalled the blunt threats he'd issued to Linton after paying the five thousand pounds for Iris's hand in marriage. Relegating the lord to the country where he'd be kept under lock and key. Shipping him off to New South Wales. Anything to deter the man from leeching off Clarke's fortune as his father-in-law.

Foolish, really. He'd known men who couldn't resist a bet no matter what the cost, and the same fanatical gleam lived in Linton's rheumy eyes.

"Perhaps you should have been more forceful, then, because he lost two thousand pounds to Oliver Johnson last night."

"Oliver Johnson? What the hell is he doing in town?" Johnson used to be a part of their group until he'd slept with a former paramour of Clarke's. While he hadn't harbored deep feelings for the woman—her cheating hardly dented his ego—he refused to trust Johnson again. If a man couldn't trust his friend around his mistress, how could he be expected to trust him in business?

"Just arrived from Boston and wanted to shoot the breeze with an old friend," Porter explained. "I know how you feel about him, and I don't blame you. But he's apologized, and I genuinely think he means it. Surely, that's all water under the bridge now, anyway. It's been five years, and you're married."

"The man proved himself untrustworthy. He can take his apology and shove it up his arse."

Porter reclined in his chair and shook his head. "I knew you'd react this way, which is why I wasn't going to tell you he was in London. Except we ran into Linton, and... Well, now it appears you'll owe Johnson those two thousand pounds if you're wanting to avoid more trouble for your wife's father."

"Fuck."

"My sentiments exactly." Sighing, Porter packed away the rest of their work as the maid finished wiping away the last of the fallen ink. Clinking glass rang in the room, amber liquid pouring from a large bottle into two tumblers. "Unfortunately, Linton and Johnson were already deep in play when I arrived or else I would've warned Oliver to leave the man alone."

The alcohol burned a path down Clarke's throat after he accepted a glass from Porter. Like a thorn in a lion's paw, Linton presented a constant blight to his previously amiable life. With the profits from two hotels and a third about to be built, along with his other business endeavors, Clarke didn't fear being paupered but did object to having his hard-earned money thrown away as easily as rubbish in the bin.

His skin chafed where he scrubbed a hand over his roughened cheek, the discomfort echoing the friction between him and his father-in-law. "I'm not sure what to do. If I had my way, Linton would be on the first conveyance out of London, but Iris is determined to make the man into some kind of 'Father of the Year'. She wants to make up for all the years they've missed out on, despite the marquess's distinct lack of interest."

"Ah, the trials and tribulations of marriage," Porter mused, balancing his half-empty glass on his knee. "Have you tried explaining to her the benefits of removing the man from temptation?"

"Of course not. She doesn't need to be burdened further with his absolute failure as a decent person." Seeing the dimming of her light after brief interactions with her father was enough. Each day when she returned from setting his house to rights, her eyes looked a little sadder, her face a little more strained. Clarke would've loved to forbid her from wasting her precious time on the old lord but doubted her acceptance of such a decree.

Especially since she fought so hard to be the one to get her father's home back into working order.

"Good to hear that communication is alive and well in your relationship." A wry laugh erupted from his friend, and Clarke shot him a very ungentlemanly gesture with his finger.

Wait until you're married...

Unholy glee flared at the thought. Yes, Clarke would definitely remember to tease Porter just as mercilessly upon that day.

Until then, however, he'd have to tolerate his friend's teasing while navigating the often confusing waters of marriage. *Which is why you scheduled a block of time later this afternoon for your little problem-solving session.* He may not come up with anything useful, but it felt good to have a plan—even a vague one.

Because he had feelings for Iris.

He wanted to bed her desperately.

But he was also a behemoth who wasn't used to tempering his lovemaking.

And he had a fragile mother who worried him constantly—somehow, he needed to figure out how to *not* place Iris in that same frail category.

Ands, buts, alsos... His list of concerns grew until he waved his tumbler towards Porter, silently asking for another drink.

He'd need it for the job ahead.

CHAPTER ELEVEN

I*'m late. I'm late.*

The litany pushed Iris to a greater pace as she hurried to finish sewing the buttons on her father's coat. After her and Clarke's agreement, she'd hired staff to run the kitchen, clean each room, and take care of general tidying—such as sewing on lost buttons—but when Linton personally asked her to fix this jacket...

She couldn't deny him.

Why couldn't he ask a maid?

Because apparently this jacket has been passed down for generations, and he didn't want a stranger to accidentally ruin it.

So, here she sat frantically pulling a needle and thread through his cuff, praying to be done while avoiding pricking her finger and bleeding all over the white fabric. It was a flimsy reason for having her sew on a couple of buttons and not especially worth upsetting her husband—*yet here I am because I couldn't refuse Linton.*

She cursed her weakness. And the time it was taking her to complete the task.

Because tonight was important. Clarke's friends and business associates were gathering for a soiree, and she'd finally get a look inside her husband's world. She couldn't afford to make a bad impression or embarrass him, especially now that they were on firmer ground since their night in the library, despite the hiccup of distance between them directly afterwards.

He'd shared about his family. She'd reciprocated—overcoming her initial stammering and shyness—and it felt like a relationship was truly flourishing between them.

Don't forget about the kiss in the foyer.

A dreamy sigh fell from her lips as her fingers paused their work. Clarke had been so gentle with her. So tender. The imprint of his lips upon hers remained carved into her memory, slipping into dreams of love and happily-ever-after. Lily and Caraway liked to tease her and Hazel about their hopeless romantic outlook on life, but Hazel had found her Prince Charming in a rookery rogue despite their warnings. Perhaps her happiness resided in someone just as unexpected—a dark-haired scoundrel, according to her sisters, who'd paid for her hand in marriage.

Either way, Iris didn't want to derail their progress by arriving tardy to an event with Clarke, one where she'd be on display as a reflection of him. Her performance at the Taft dinner for Linton had been mediocre at best. It couldn't happen again with Clarke.

These people are different, though. Nouveau riche. Surely, they won't be as snooty about bloodlines or as intrusive.

Iris prayed that would be true.

"Ma'am, Jimmy's outside saying it's time to leave if you're wanting to have time to prepare yourself properly for this evening's dinner." A young maid popped her head into the room, a nervous air about her.

"Thank you, Emily. Tell him I'll be right out." Biting off a bit of loose thread after tying off the final knot, Iris folded the old jacket and set it aside. *I should've taken this home to sew.* Feeling silly for risking Clarke's bad opinion over a request from her father, she berated her thoughtlessness, blaming her tangled emotions for the oversight. "Could you return Lord Linton's coat to his room, please? I've finished adding new buttons and would do it myself but with Jimmy—"

"It's alright, ma'am. I'll do it happily, and I could've done the sewing, too. You only need to ask."

"I know, but it was a personal request of my father." Gathering her hat and gloves from the front table in the foyer, Iris waved goodbye before scurrying down the steps, skirt in hand, casting a grateful glance towards Jimmy, who held the carriage door open for her. Thank goodness his fall had only resulted in bruising and minor cuts which only kept him abed for an evening before insisting he was healthy enough to continue working. "I apologize for the long wait, Jimmy. Please make haste on our way home. I don't want to upset Mr. Calloway with my delayed arrival."

"I wouldn't worry about him, ma'am. He gets all red in the face like a schoolboy with a crush whenever you're near. And I know for a fact he'd tell me to go slow for your safety rather than fast for time's sake, so that's what I'm going to do." Jimmy tugged on his hat in a gesture of respect before hopping atop the carriage and leaving her slack-jawed at the bevy of details just revealed.

Clarke with a schoolboy crush? On her?

Well, did you think he kissed every woman with such tenderness?

Relaxing into her seat, Iris watched the city go by as she happily imagined a flustered Clarke full of emotions for her. It meant the plan she'd haphazardly hatched on their wedding day was working—he was falling for her, after all.

What a relief to learn her heart wasn't the only one involved.

While she couldn't admit to being fully in love with her husband yet, Iris knew she was well on her way because it was impossible to keep her feelings from developing in the wake of Clarke's kindness and generosity. Most men might have continued with their plan of exploiting her illegitimacy to Society. Most would seek to get their money's worth from her.

But Clarke hadn't been able to follow through with such callous treatment. What's more, he'd confessed to his underhanded agenda and apologized for it. It took a strong man to expose his mistakes and atone for them. Not that she expected much in the way of atonement. He'd dismissed the idea before it ever came to fruition, but that didn't stop him from gifting her with jewelry, flower arrangements, and even the funds to staff her father's home.

If only he'd gift you with his presence in your bed.

The unladylike thought brought a secretive smile to her lips as the carriage stopped in front of her home a quarter hour later. *In due time.* She contented herself with the promise. Already they were making headway with an increased frequency of kisses. Sharing the marriage bed couldn't be too far off.

Exiting the carriage with light feet, Iris flew into the foyer and up the stairs, almost making it to her bedchamber before ramming into a solid form when rounding the balustrade.

Burly arms wrapped around her waist, and she found herself swiftly lifted in the air and deposited in the hall as if she were a dandelion caught on the wind.

"Careful, you almost knocked yourself back down the stairs. What's the rush?"

"The dinner party." She tried catching her breath, but the air tingled with Clarke's tart lemon scent, which flustered her even more. "I'm sorry for taking so long getting home. I told Jimmy to hurry, but he refused to listen."

"As he should have. You're far more precious than a party," Clarke said, large hands soothing up and down her arms. "Besides, knowing my friends, we won't be the only couple arriving fashionably late."

"Are you sure? I don't want to make a bad first impression."

"Darling, no one could ever think badly of you. If they don't wax poetic over your beauty first, then they'll remark upon your lovely disposition." With the amount of compliments she was receiving today, she'd be lucky if they didn't comment on her giant ego, but Iris let his words sink in, reveling in the knowledge that he found her *beautiful, lovely*.

"Speaking of which... I have a gift for you in my room. Shall I fetch it while you change into something more festive?"

Glancing down at her wrinkled cotton dress, she figured she must look a fright after pitching in to help some of the maids shift furniture to remove and clean the rugs. "That sounds perfect. I'll see you soon." On impulse, Iris steadied herself with hands on Clarke's waist and reached up to brush a kiss over his upturned mouth, catching his smile with her lips.

See? Progress.

A month ago, she never would've felt comfortable enough to kiss her husband in an open display of affection. And Iris doubted Clarke would've clung so firmly to her waist—reciprocating in earnest the spontaneous embrace—considering his decision to keep her at a safe distance from his *bear paws*. A moniker she refused to use when it came to his large, rough-hewn palms because she quite enjoyed their coarse texture smoothing along her skin.

Upon entering her chamber, Iris quickly changed into a peach satin gown with the help of Edith before sending the girl away as she waited for Clarke's arrival. Tonight would be the perfect time to bestow him with her own gift, she decided. Iris had just retrieved the present from its hiding place in her armoire when a knock sounded on the door.

"Come in."

Muted footsteps followed the summons until Clarke saw her and immediately paused in the middle of the room. "How beautiful you are, little sprite."

A hot blush rose at the compliment, and Iris shyly drifted nearer. "You're quite handsome yourself... Though, you're missing the final touch to complete your ensemble."

"Oh?" His lips tipped upward in amused confusion as he reached out to trace the lace trim along her bodice.

Shivering at the intimate contact, she nodded, swallowing hard at the sudden dryness in her throat. For some reason, the notion of giving him a gift made her nervous. What if he disliked it? Thought it too forward?

You're husband and wife, not a maiden with her beau. It's perfectly respectable.

Besides, it wasn't as if she bought him anything scandalous.

"Yes... I... um... This is for you." She thrust the decorative box into his hand and cursed her stammering. *So much for a romantic declaration to accompany it.*

"And this is yours." Clarke presented the velvet case in his other hand with a flourish, which she gratefully accepted, happy to have a distraction while he opened her gift. He removed the gold pocket watch from its safe perch and let it twirl on its chain as he examined it.

"I had it engraved... on the back. It's the day of our—"

"Wedding," he finished for her, appreciation lighting his dark eyes. Without hesitation, he replaced the pocket watch he wore with the new one, his thumb brushing back and forth across the inscription.

"I know we didn't meet in the usual way of couples, but I wanted to show you that I don't regret marrying you. In fact... I think I would've chosen you even if Linton hadn't interfered. If we happened to ever meet in London, that is..." Iris stumbled over her words, feeling silly for voicing such a thing. They never would've met. They came from different worlds—worlds that meant their paths wouldn't have crossed by pure happenstance.

"I'd have chosen you, too, sprite." A rumble in his chest punctuated the claim as he wrapped a large hand around her neck and drew her up for a brutal kiss. One of ownership. Possession. Passion.

Burying her hands in his hair while she had a chance—before he thought to restrain her—Iris poured every emotion she held in her heart into the embrace, resolute in pushing him over the edge of control. The dinner party lay forgotten in the wake of their admissions. The present in her hand fell to the carpet, cast aside in favor of caressing her husband.

Iris wanted to savor this moment.

Wanted it to propel them into finally consummating their marriage.

Unfortunately, it wasn't meant to be. Clarke retreated, gently disentangling her arms from around his neck before sweetly kissing her forehead. His labored breathing matched her own, his thick arousal a physical display to mimic the dampness between her thighs. "As much as I adore kissing you, I'm afraid we must quit while ahead. We're expected tonight, and I know how you were looking forward to meeting my friends."

Yes, she had been quite excited. But that was before she had a chance to make love with her husband.

"We could always attend the next event..."

Chuckling, Clarke nipped at the inside of her wrist before releasing her to pick up his fallen gift—a necklace, according to the splayed jewels peeking out of the popped-open box. "Tempting... very tempting... Here, let me put this on you, then we can leave. Or I suppose I should check it goes with your outfit first?"

"It's fine." Iris presented her back to him and shifted her hair to the side as he brought the ornate necklace around her neck. Even if they clashed horribly, she would've worn the dress and accessory together. Her flustered emotions wouldn't have allowed any other option. "Tell me what I should know about the people I'll be meeting tonight."

She figured if Clarke wouldn't skip the party altogether, she might as well distract herself with details about his friends. Perhaps it would cool some of the ardor heating her blood.

Unlikely, but worth a try.

A FEW HOURS LATER, after she'd met a multitude of guests and smiled so much her cheeks hurt, a lilting voice drifted across the room to compliment Iris. "I adore your necklace, dear. A gift from your husband?"

Beaming in Clarke's direction, oblivious to the tightening around his mouth, Iris nodded at Mrs. Ronda's comment. A gorgeous widow, she flitted around the room like Queen Cleopatra herself, despite not being the official hostess of the party. "Yes, he's extremely generous."

The gift he'd bestowed upon her earlier in the evening lay sparkling along her décolletage, sapphires glinting under the chandelier light. It was extravagant and wholly unnecessary given the amount of jewelry he'd previously given her, but Iris knew her husband showed his care through gift giving, so she accepted every expensive trinket and bauble with a grateful smile and a flutter in her heart. Besides, it also commemorated a lovely confession.

He'd choose me as his wife, with no strings attached.

A choking cough erupted at her right from Mr. Porter while Mrs. Ronda smirked, her red lips twisting in triumph. "Oh, I wholeheartedly agree. Very generous indeed." Her pink-tipped nails traced the elaborate design of emeralds and diamonds draping her neck, and suddenly Iris had the odd feeling of being caught in a spider's web, an undertone of malice shading the seemingly polite conversation.

"Oh, leave the poor girl alone, Lavinia." The man across from Iris playfully rapped Mrs. Ronda's knuckles with his. "Let's move on to more entertaining topics... What do we think of this past edition of Presley's Papers?" he asked, referencing a periodical devoted solely to gossip.

The evening was proving extremely enlightening to Iris as she learned the inner workings of another social circle she'd never dreamed of entering. From open discussions of business to philosophical debates between men and women, it almost felt like the lively conversations her family would have around the fire in Hampshire—though they mostly centered around whatever story Hazel was writing or the latest botanical development her parents had discovered, rather than political or social gossip.

But while Iris valued the mass of knowledge bandying about the room, there was one bit of information she wished she could've ignored. The palpable connection some of the women felt with Clarke. Logically, it didn't surprise her; he was a handsome man, after all. However, she hadn't expected his past... *acquaintances* to be so transparent about their relationship, to wear their desire so plainly for everyone—including his wife—to see.

Perhaps I'm imagining it.

Don't be naïve.

When guests began their journey towards the drawing room for entertainment, Iris took the opportunity to question Clarke about Mrs. Ronda in particular, as she was the most vocal about her attachment. *Best to expose the truth and move past it, instead of driving yourself into a fit over wondering.*

Her voice hovered around a whisper as she asked, "Mrs. Ronda. She's a former... paramour of yours?" The guess didn't seem too outrageous based on the envious looks the woman shot Iris's way and the oblique comments alluding to private knowledge she had of Clarke, which Iris would never be privy to.

"Yes."

Confirmation.

Finding the beautiful lady ahead of them, scarlet skirts swishing across the floor, shiny black curls bouncing along her shoulders, Iris contemplated this past liaison of her husband's. A twinge of jealousy sprouted in her gut, but the strongest emotion leaned towards reluctant acceptance.

Now, I know. At least he didn't lie.

"She's very beautiful. I understand the attraction."

Quiet chatter infiltrated the silence between them until he cleared his throat, tugging on his collar. "You're handling her presence remarkably well."

"Did you expect me to throw a tantrum in front of your friends?"

"No, but most women would make some snide comment. Or give me the cold shoulder for the rest of the evening. I suppose I should've known you'd take it in stride, as you've taken every trial tossed your way lately."

"While people like to compare me to innocent, mythical creatures like fairies or *sprites*..." Iris pinned him with a pointed stare. "I am, in truth, a flesh and blood woman. And while the monikers don't bother me mostly—I'm not blind to my physical attributes—I also don't want to be put on a pedestal because of it. I'm stronger and wiser than I look," she concluded with a huff. "Which means I don't fault you for having a past."

Properly reprimanded, their entwined arms allowed him to pull her close enough for him to whisper in her ear. "Duly noted, wife. Though I apologize for Lavinia's presence. Had I known she'd be here, I would've had us skip this event for the next one, after all. Because however sophisticated you are, little sprite, I don't want my past tainting you."

She laughed at the notion, drawing the attention of several guests. "I believe it's the other way around. My past is tarnishing *your* future. I know Linton isn't your favorite person. I can tell by the way your eyes narrow every time he enters the room." He opened his mouth to refute the accusation, but Iris patted his hand in empathy. "No, don't deny it. I don't hold it against you. I just wanted to make the point that my past is the one causing trouble, not yours."

Clarke seemed to search for a rebuttal, his gaze meeting hers before glancing away, his jaw working as if preparing to speak, only to pause as he rethought. Finally, he stopped them before following the procession into a brightly lit room where guests were already circling a piano and flipping through sheet music. "You're too good for me, little sprite." There was a softness in his amber eyes that matched the tone of his voice, and the hope of earning his love rose again, flamed higher by the tenderness Iris saw.

He didn't wait for a response, leading her inside to a prime seat on a chaise lounge, his body dwarfing hers as he sat by her side. One by one, guests offered to play or sing a song—some wonderfully full of talent while others only sought a laugh at their antics—and Iris floated in the jovial atmosphere, warm and content with her husband's heat seeping through their layers of clothing to spark along her nerves.

Oh, how she needed him.

Kisses were special, each sweeter than the last, but Iris yearned for an encore of their wedding night... or even the night in the library window. Of Clarke's fingertips roaming over her skin, exploring parts of her no one else had ever known. But those same fingertips were the barrier between them because they left purple marks behind on her hips, her thighs. Brands Iris would proudly wear again, except her husband mistakenly believed he harmed her in some way, despite her pleas to the contrary.

She wanted his imprint on her body again.

She needed that strong anchor he provided, grounding her in a way she'd never felt before.

But how to convince him of her durability?

The true conundrum.

"Would you like a drink? They're calling for an interlude before starting up again, and I think we can use some liquid fortification." Agreeing absent-mindedly, Iris watched Clarke head towards a refreshment table set up on the other side of the room. A tower of champagne glasses formed a precarious pyramid, while colorful macarons surrounded the base. Though separated by generations of wealth and bloodlines, this group of people looked a lot like those at the Taft dinner—richly dressed men and women who had money to spare.

"Mrs. Calloway, have you met Mr. Oliver Johnson?" Mrs. Ronda appeared to her right, a handsome man with green eyes staring down at Iris. She promptly rose from her seat to avoid the feeling of being dominated in some strange way.

"You know she hasn't, Lav." A smooth voice greeted her from above. "Or else I'd remember because you're very pretty." He winked, bowed, and gallantly held out a hand for hers as if he meant to kiss it like a knight of old. "And I can never resist a pretty girl—"

The punch came out of nowhere.

An ominous growl followed, then Clarke stood over a bleeding Mr. Johnson, panting in fury, while screams of shock rose from the women in the room and the men descended upon them, eager to witness the blood sport.

Iris met her husband's wild eyes amongst the chaos, and the pure fire ignited in their depths would've charred anyone within standing distance. As its closest recipient, she felt the lick of heat travel through her veins to settle between her thighs.

This man reminded her of the ferocity of the lover from their wedding night.

Man turned feral beast who only she could tame.

But can *you tame such a wild creature?*

CHAPTER TWELVE

C larke never ran from a fight.
Growing up near the docks, a rougher crowd ruled the streets, and he made sure to always be on guard. To learn how to protect himself and his mum when his father was off at sea.

However, it'd been a long time since he'd been a boy forced to defend a delicate woman. These days, he avoided such entanglements because they always turned messy.

Case in point?

His former friend lying on the floor, staining the floral carpet beneath him with blood and tears. Well, tears may have been an exaggeration, but they wouldn't be remiss in Clarke's mind.

When he'd returned to find Johnson speaking with Iris—trying to charm her—his vision saw red. He became a charging bull in a Spanish arena.

No one touched his wife.

Least of all a bastard like Johnson.

"Boys, must we resort to fisticuffs over a woman? How positively medieval." Lavinia's snide remark darted from the left as she knelt to help Johnson.

"Blame, Calloway. He's the one who has a problem with someone greeting his wife," Johnson spit out, hauling himself to his feet. "I find it curious I didn't warrant a blow to the head after what happened with me and Virginia, yet you see me within a hands-breadth of your wife and see fit to flatten me to the ground. Perhaps medieval is too generous, Lav. Perhaps we need to go further back to the time of Neanderthals."

"I'll do more than that if you come near Iris again," Clarke warned, uncaring of the scene being made. Gossip swarmed from guest to guest like a beehive brimming with industry. By tomorrow, the whole of London would hear of Mr. Calloway's frightening display of rage and jealousy.

But he didn't give a damn.

All he cared about was keeping Johnson's paws off of Iris, then stealing her away for himself.

One task done. Time to see to the other.

"Threatening me over a woman? Porter was right. You really have changed."

Porter had the grace to look guilty for speaking about him with a man he knew Clarke loathed.

"Maybe I have, but you certainly haven't." Turning to their hosts, he dipped his head in farewell before pulling Iris into him. "I believe this is our cue to leave. Thank you for dinner, and please send me a bill for the rug if it's irreparably ruined."

Light taps trailed his booted stomps out of the room, down the corridor, and straight to the foyer, where he called for their outer garments and carriage. His skin felt too tight, like leather left too long in the sun for curing. At any moment, he might crack, and there was no telling what might burst forth.

"Who—" Iris started, but he held a hand up.

"Not yet. Let... let me calm down for a second." He paced back and forth, an animal trapped in too close of quarters.

Oliver fucking Johnson. Even thinking the man's name had Clarke wanting to race back to the parlor and deck him again for daring to speak to Iris.

His wife.

Ten minutes later, their carriage arrived ready for their departure and Iris and Clarke took opposite sides of the comfortable cab as it proceeded towards home. *Dammit, now I'm caged in here, too.* He unbuttoned his collar, which helped his lungs drag in deeper gulps of air, then tugged off his jacket and rolled up his sleeves, too hot under all the layers.

"Who was that man? And who was Virginia?" Iris tried asking again, and he gave her credit for bravery. His little sprite hadn't lied earlier—she was stronger than he gave her credit for. *At least in spirit*, he thought as his gaze devoured her tiny form mere inches from him.

"Oliver Johnson, former friend and almost business partner. He fucked a mistress of mine before I was done with her. After that, I couldn't trust him, so I cut him out of a business deal. He's been in America until recently."

"I'm sorry for his betrayal... and your mistress's," she murmured. "You lost two people you cared for in the most callous way possible."

"Save your sympathy. My heart wasn't broken by Virginia nor by Johnson. In fact, he saved me from making the mistake of going into business with him—something that would've been a hassle to get out of after we'd signed contracts and the like."

A silver lining in retrospect.

The carriage rocked over a dip in the road, causing Iris to jerk forward, her breasts pushing against the fabric of her dress, dangerously close to spilling out. Clarke clamped his hands around her upper thighs, his breath fanning over the exposed skin of her chest. "Steady, sprite. Wouldn't want to take a tumble, would you?"

Unless it's the metaphorical kind, of course.

Her hands curled around his shoulders as he eased down to his knees. Voluminous skirts tangled around his legs. Her heady scent weaved through his senses, and the chaotic energy riding him from the altercation with Johnson found its outlet.

Their kiss at home flashed through his mind. Her considerate gift. Her sweet declaration.

She'd choose me.

And it was enough to toss him into the crashing waves of lust and desire.

Damn the consequences.

Clarke shoved the skirt of her gown higher, his mouth falling to her stocking-covered knee, the heat of his breath sending a thrill through Iris. But she was tired of only receiving. She wanted to know her husband's pleasure, as well.

"Wait, wait. Clarke." Iris rapped on his shoulder, urging him back. A disgruntled expression highlighted his features, the fire of earlier barely banked in the depths of his dark eyes.

"What's wrong? You don't want this?"

"No. I want it very much, but I don't want it alone. I want to touch you, too." The quiet admission tumbled out in the jostling carriage, and her husband looked stunned. Was it so strange for a wife to desire such a thing? She doubted her sisters kept to themselves with as often as she'd caught a caress to a cheek here or a squeeze of a leg there.

Rocking back on his heels, Clarke mumbled something under his breath—an epithet, a prayer? —before sitting beside her. "You want to touch me?"

"Yes, if it's alright..." His slow acceptance made her wary. Weren't men supposed to be filled with animal spirits? Controlled by their lusts? Iris wanted him as eager for her attention as she was for his.

"We don't have much time. Are you sure this is what you want?"

"I'm positive." She'd dreamed of nothing else for weeks. Imagining the feel of him after witnessing his arousal encased in trim trousers upon several occasions. Only hours ago, she thought her wish might come true, and now here they were again, on the precipice.

Their heavy breathing filled the cabin, steaming the windows with the passion of its occupants, and Iris waited for Clarke's instruction.

"Since we'll be home any minute, this will be quick and dirty." He paused as if she'd suddenly clam up like a nun in a brothel, but she just nodded, skin tingling with anticipation. Quick? Not ideal. But dirty? A wicked part of her looked forward to it.

"Undo my trousers and pull my cock out. You're going to stroke it with those soft little hands of yours while I pump your cunt with my fingers. Understand?"

"I think so—" He didn't let her finish the sentence, covering her mouth with his own in a savage kiss as his hand dove under her skirts again, unerringly finding the slit of her drawers to immediately circle the budding pearl of her sex.

Gasping at the abrupt attack, Iris fumbled with the buttons of Clarke's trousers, intent on not being left behind.

I'll prove that I can please him.

The engorged stalk of his arousal leapt into her palm, scalding her with its heat. Thick and long, it matched its owner's enormous size, and for the first time, Iris wondered if perhaps Clarke didn't have a point about going slow with her. It seemed outrageous that he'd fit inside her. His massive cock and her tiny body—they appeared incompatible.

I'll concern myself with logistics later.

For now, they were on borrowed time as Jimmy drove them down a deserted street, and Iris hesitantly began stroking Clarke.

"Harder, sprite. Like this." One of his hands enclosed hers, the both of them squeezing and sliding down his cock in tandem, all the while his other hand continued its rhythmic circling of her clit. She thought the manic way he forced his cock through their tight grips too harsh, but he groaned and jerked, each coarse sound flooding her mouth as Clarke's kiss turned almost punishing.

They rode over a bumpy portion of the road, Clarke's fingers pounding deeper against a particularly sensitive spot inside, and Iris's body arched into his, a muted scream of pleasure lodged in her throat. Her fingers went lax underneath Clarke's, but it didn't matter. He kept brutal command over his cock until a jet of warm seed soaked their hands, his growl of satisfaction ringing in her ears.

Kissing his cheeks and neck with lazy abandon, Iris basked in the afterglow of their lovemaking. She'd enjoyed Clarke's generosity in the library, but this surpassed even that intimate moment. Because they'd come together. There was mutual exchange of affection—*of love* if Iris were honest with herself.

A handkerchief swept across her palm to clean off the remnants of Clarke's release, and she reveled in the tender care her husband took of her body after such a storm of passion. He worried about being too much for her. Placed too high of an importance on her tiny stature.

But perhaps tonight was the first step in changing his mind. In asserting her strength as a grown woman.

"Was that what you wanted, sprite?" he asked as their carriage began to slow.

"Mhmm..." She nodded, brushing another kiss across his heated skin, just because she could. "Yes, quick and dirty suits me."

Another epithet from him, this time marginally louder. "You'll be the death of me, I swear."

Iris forced herself to straighten, ensuring she looked presentable when Jimmy opened the carriage door. "A little sprite like me felling a sturdy oak like yourself? I doubt it." And feeling especially shameless after their lovemaking, she winked, giggling at the endearing moan of forbearance Clarke exhaled.

"I realize you're mocking my concerns about our size difference, but never doubt your power over me. Even the mountainside is shaped by the gentle passing of a river."

Before she could reply, they were home with Jimmy waiting for them to disembark from the carriage. Clarke guided her inside the brownstone and upstairs to her room, but when Iris tried pulling him inside to continue their lovemaking uninterrupted, he stopped her.

"Not yet, love."

"But I thought..." His withdrawal baffled her. Surely, he didn't still think her too weak to handle his desire.

Clarke sighed. "I know. But we're not ready to proceed that far yet. This evening was an anomaly because of Johnson's presence. I let him under my skin, and I couldn't control the outburst that followed."

"So did I. I'm healthy and whole, in one piece, despite your worries." She held out her arms as if for inspection. "You don't need to keep such a tight leash on yourself, Clarke. I won't break. I promise."

His large palms tenderly cupped her cheeks, regret cloaking his features. "I'm sorry, but I'm not willing to risk it. Not yet, anyway. We need more time, and I need to figure out the best way forward." He brushed a featherlight kiss over her lips before retreating. "Now go to bed, sprite. *Please.*"

It was the desperate note of begging in his voice that convinced her to let it go. She didn't want to force him into something he didn't want. He needed to make peace with whatever misgivings he had, and unfortunately, that meant Iris had to wait.

Patience had always been a virtue of hers, but in this case, she loathed its necessity.

"Okay... Good night, Clarke." Iris briefly touched a hand to his heart, then closed the door to her room. It would be a long time, though, before sleep claimed her.

CHAPTER THIRTEEN

"I f you're available, my mum would like to meet you, and since I'm visiting her today..." Clarke trailed off the next day as he entered the parlor, uncertainty written on his expression. He wore a suit of lightweight trousers and a gray jacket with subtle stripes patterning the fabric. The obvious effort made to appear impeccably groomed for his mother caused her to stumble a little in her haste to stand and agree to his proposition. Meeting the elder Mrs. Calloway had been on her list of wishes once she realized the woman hadn't attended her only son's wedding.

A mystery, to be sure.

Her only piece of knowledge about the woman came from Clarke when he'd mentioned his parents being a love match, otherwise, she remained clueless as to what the woman who'd raised Iris's husband was like.

"I would love to meet your mother." The clock struck two in the afternoon, and another mystery seemed on the cusp of being solved. "Is this where you go every week on Wednesdays? To visit your mother?"

"Noticed that, did you? I wasn't hiding her or anything. It's just... I wasn't prepared for the two of you to meet yet." Red flushed from his neck to his cheeks like a child caught in the midst of mischief. "But Mum warned me to bring you today or else, and I'd rather not discover what she'd plan as retribution for disobeying her edict."

"Smart woman." Iris patted his shoulder as she walked by, eschewing gloves and hat for the day, rather looking forward to the freedom of the sun on her bare head and hands. In Hampshire, she'd never been so formal in her attire, but London required different expectations of its citizens.

Not to mention a marquess's daughter. Even illegitimate ones.

Though fatigue had plagued her all morning due to a restless night, Iris felt buoyed by an impending visit with her mother-in-law. The drive to a beautiful terraced house covered in ivy took half an hour, and Clarke spent the entirety of the time waffling between nervous silence—his hands fiddling with a stray thread or loose hair—and explaining his mother's health condition—angina of the heart which kept her tired and easily winded if she became too excited.

Sometimes he'd pause after listing a symptom and check for a reaction, as if expecting her to order the carriage back home in horror. Clearly, his protective nature stemmed from caring for his ailing mother, and Iris felt herself slide a little further down the road to love, captivated by this side of her husband.

When they arrived at his mother's home, a friendly woman named Maude greeted them and assured Clarke that "Mrs. Calloway is in fine shape this afternoon," before leading them to a room filled with cheerful light and yellow pastels decorating the curtains, paintings, and furniture.

"Mum, I've brought someone with me today. Shall I make introductions?" Wrapping his strong arms around a woman sitting before a fire, he teased her with a cheeky grin. Mrs. Calloway affectionately wiggled his ear before nodding.

"Of course, my boy! Don't make an old woman wait! I want to see my beautiful daughter-in-law."

"Sprite?" Clarke reached out for her, and she glided forward to place her hand in his as he pulled her into view. "Mum, this is my wife, Iris."

"Oh, but you're as pretty as a picture, and please call me Pru or Mum when you're comfortable. Now, why don't you tell me about yourself, dear? Clarke said you're from Hampshire? London must be a great change from what you're used to." The older woman smiled and gestured to the settee across from her, urging them to sit down while she requested more refreshments from Maude, who'd waited in the background while introductions were made.

Iris launched into descriptions of the small village of Shoreham and her family cottage, extolling the virtues of the countryside before moving on to her sisters and their unique characteristics. Pru encouraged every story with exclamations of delight or curious questions, and it occurred to her that Linton had never expressed such interest. Clarke's mother now knew more about her life after a quarter of an hour than her own father did in the weeks of their acquaintance.

Regretting the indulgence of that last lemon tart, Iris placed a calming hand on her stomach, willing the onset of melancholy to dissipate. Today wasn't about her relationship with Linton. It's meant to build a bridge between her and Pru.

Two new parents in quick succession.

She slammed the door on the guilty thought as soon as it appeared. *They aren't replacements for Mama and Papa.* But her gut twisted at the implication—not to mention the unfairness to her sisters. *Lily has Owen's mother, and you don't begrudge her that relationship. Why should they feel any different towards you?*

"What an incredible tale to learn you're of noble origins," Pru said, lifting her teacup, then pausing after realizing it was empty and setting it aside. "A marquess's daughter, how lovely... And your children will share the same blood. I'll have noble grandchildren! Can you imagine?"

Iris couldn't. Her dreams of family had faded into hibernation while sorting through her feelings for Clarke and Linton, but the reminder of their potential future as parents sent a hopeful thrill through her veins.

"You and grandchildren..." The exasperated muttering came from Clarke as he got up to tuck a falling knitted blanket tighter around his mother's frail knees and refill her cup of tea. Witnessing such tender care between the two threatened to overwhelm her as unexpected tears surfaced. Their relationship looked nothing like hers and Linton's. Granted, their bond grew under very different circumstances, but Iris couldn't help a spot of envy—and grief at her loss of Mama and Papa with whom she'd shared a similar closeness.

The reasoning behind his fears over her frailty became clearer, and she understood why he took her safety so seriously. He was a natural protector. His muscled form could easily lean towards brute force, but he harnessed that power and channeled it into defending those he considered weaker than him.

Perhaps she should balk at falling into that category, but a fluttery part of her body reveled in the attention. A peculiar side effect of seeing this side of her husband—the clenching warmth settling low in her belly.

Last evening's rushed lovemaking in the carriage rose in her mind, and Iris fought to maintain her composure.

You're with his mother, for goodness's sake!

Taking a fortifying sip of her own tea, Iris began another tale of Hampshire, focusing on the kind woman before her instead of the alluring presence of her husband.

"Shall I share the time my sister Hazel had us all dress as forest animals for one of her stories? Lily made quite the porcupine..."

Pru chuckled at the description—full of enthusiasm for more anecdotes of the Taylor family—but as more time passed, her energy began wilting under such excitement, and soon Maude came to help her mistress to bed for a lie-down after Clarke and Iris said their goodbyes.

"Your mother is lovely. It's a shame her ailment prevents her from doing much more than knitting or reading. She seems like the type of woman who'd love to attend soirees and picnics, all sorts of get-togethers, and she'd be the life of the party." They'd chosen to walk a little since the weather was so nice, as Jimmy followed behind with the carriage at a sedate pace. Other couples passed with brief greetings of hello, while Clarke ensured she remained safely by his side with him between her and the street.

"Thank you. She adored you, too." He squeezed the hand she had on his arm. "I've often wished she was free to enjoy the life she imagines in her head. I've tried enlisting many a physician's help to no avail, so I content myself by regaling her with tales of extravagant balls and Society gossip. It's a poor substitute, but she doesn't seem to mind. And now she has the outlandish stories of your sisters. Quite the little hellions, hmmm?"

Pinching his forearm, Iris gasped in mock indignation. "Excuse me, sir, but you've gotten the wrong impression. The Taylors of Hampshire are nothing but upstanding, genteel women."

"Ah, I must have missed the part of that definition which includes girls dressing as porcupines and poking unsuspecting villagers with their quills."

"All part of an elaborate story about redemption and—" Iris couldn't continue any longer without bursting into laughter. Hazel and Lily had definitely been hellions. "Oh, dash it, you're correct in your assessment, dear husband, but don't let my sisters know I agree with you."

"Never." Clarke crossed his heart with all the seriousness of a priest during mass. "It falls under the confidentiality between a husband and wife."

She liked the sound of that—a shared vault of secrets only the two of them were privy to, an intimate strengthening of their marital bond. "Excellent! Then I suppose I'm free to share our concerns about Caraway with you, and perhaps you can provide a solution."

"Is your sister ailing?"

"No, no! Nothing like that... My sisters and I are just determined to see her happily married like the rest of us. We were hopeful that our broadened circle of possible gentlemen matches would aid our endeavor, but Lily's written how Cara doesn't seem interested when she proposes potential events to meet actual suitors. And we're afraid it's because of Miles

Brandon." Iris didn't know the man well. He'd always been Owen's family friend. However, it was obvious whenever he was around that Cara became acutely attuned to his presence.

The change he wrought in her usually practical sister would've delighted Iris if it weren't for the rumors Lily had shared with her about his careless past with women and how even Owen maintained the friendship out of a sense of duty rather than affection.

"And how would you like me to help?" Clarke asked as they dodged an exuberant dog running from its owner. The young boy sprinted by with a flying leash zipping through the wind, a harried looking woman following behind while pushing a pram.

One of these days that could be me with our children.

"Sprite?"

Shaken from her thoughts, Iris returned to their conversation after a final glance of longing towards the family. "Do you know any eligible bachelors who may pair well with a responsible young woman? Cara's the most proper out of all of us and would make a wonderful wife and mother. My hope is if she meets the right man, she'll forget all about Brandon... Of all the times for her common sense to fail her, it *would* be with a dandy like him. They'd prove to be a terrible match."

"Love is blind, or so I've heard," Clarke drawled, patting the back of her hand. "Unfortunately, none of my friends would make suitable husbands, either. Don't forget you married a scoundrel."

"*Former* scoundrel," she corrected. "Though I see your point. Those I met at your friends' dinner don't strike me as the type for Cara—even Mr. Porter who's charm itself."

A disgruntled huff sounded beside her. "Please refrain from complimenting other men within my presence... or ever, for that matter. I'm the only man you should view as *charm itself*."

Amused by his jealousy, Iris leaned more heavily into his side, her skirts twirling around his legs, and teased, "My apologies, dear husband. Porter is an ogre compared to you. Is that better?"

"Much." An approving smirk decorated his mouth. "And as for your sister, if she's as practical as you say, then I have no doubt she'll eventually recognize Brandon's faults and move past her little crush. We can invite her to London sometime to help, perhaps stepping outside the bounds of the country—to a city where eligible men are more readily available—will aid our cause."

"I agree and..." The errant dog ran past them again, though this time the boy's pace behind him had slowed considerably. "Do you think we should help the poor lad?"

"On it." Clarke shrugged out of his jacket before handing it to her and guiding her to a shady spot under a tree to wait. "I'll catch the two ragamuffins while you wait here." He loped after the boy and dog, and Iris waved to the woman trying to keep up with her pram.

"Good afternoon! My husband has decided to enter the fray and collect your wayward wards."

"Oh, thank heavens. I'm afraid Gertrude and I are quite tired from our journey." She motioned towards a smiling baby covered in a bright yellow blanket. Iris cooed at the child while the lady continued to explain how her son's dog still hadn't mastered a leash, enjoying the fun of escaping its collar and running free.

"Quite the pup you have," Iris empathized, offering a smile of commiseration. "But don't worry, Mr. Calloway will bring the two back safely. He won't let any harm come to them."

Her husband was quite the protector, after all.

He'll be quite the father.

Seeing Clarke returning with boy and dog in tow, his arm wrapped around the child's shoulder, Iris's heart picked up speed as her hand dropped to cover her stomach. Someday they'd have children of their own, but first they needed to overcome her husband's fear of bedding her.

Not an easy feat, unfortunately.

CHAPTER FOURTEEN

An achy feeling woke Iris from her sleep later that night. Darkness held the room in a tight hold, and she groaned at the realization that dawn would be a long time coming. Rolling to her side, Iris placed a comforting hand on her abdomen, rubbing soothing circles over the cramping muscles.

Another month, another visit from mother nature.

She prayed the increasing pain would go away by itself, but after tossing and turning for another twenty minutes with no relief in sight, Iris finally gave in and got out of bed. Sleepy eyed and slightly grumpy, Iris grabbed her wrapper before heading downstairs to search out head powder for the throb burgeoning in her head along with a palliative for cramps.

Clarke's bedroom door appeared on her left as she traipsed down the hallway, and for once, their separate quarters came in handy. How embarrassing it'd be for him to find her suffering during her courses. He already believed her frail. He didn't need more physical evidence.

Entering the kitchen downstairs, she unerringly found a pan and an ewer of milk before carefully lighting the gas stove to warm a cup of the soothing liquid for herself. The exertion coupled with the onset of another symptom of her courses—overheating—caused sweat to dot her brow and the back of her neck, creating an uncomfortable itching sensation as her hair clung to the damp skin. Wetting a rag from a pitcher of water, Iris patted the damp cloth along her face and neck while stirring the milk so it wouldn't burn.

"What's going on here?" Clarke's sudden appearance sent the wooden spoon in Iris's hand clattering to the floor with a splatter of hot milk. Avoiding the splash, she hurried to retrieve another spoon, then cleaned up the mess while stealing glances at her husband. It looked like he'd recently returned from an evening out, and Iris wondered about his activities. Surely if he'd been invited to a friend's event, he'd bring his wife. Right?

Perhaps he thought you had too much excitement for one day after visiting his mother and accomplishing a rescue mission.

After dinner, Clarke had excused himself for the evening, and she'd assumed he'd retired to his study. But it seemed she was wrong.

"Warming milk. Would you like some?"

"We have help for such tasks," he said dumbly. Shirking off his jacket, he tossed it over a kitchen chair and joined her in front of the cast iron range.

Momentarily distracted, Iris placed a hand on his forehead with a mock frown. "Oh dear, have you confused me with Lady Taft or one of her ilk? Should I be concerned?" Dropping the act, she smiled and allowed her hand to drift down his cheek. "You forget I'm a country girl unused to having others do things I'm perfectly able to do myself."

"I forget nothing when it comes to you, sprite. But why are you down here at three in the morning warming milk? Are you ill?"

"Not in the usual sense..." she hedged. How to explain her monthly courses and the pain they brought without completely humiliating herself?

He's a grown man. Surely, he knows something of a woman's anatomy.

But one didn't speak openly about such matters, and Iris found it difficult to overcome the habit of keeping it private—even from her husband.

"What does that mean?"

Pouring the warmed milk into a glass, Iris returned the empty pan to the range and muttered under her breath. "It's my courses. They woke me up."

"Oh." His reaction may have been comical if she weren't already overwhelmed with mortification and throbbing cramps. Guiding her to a seat, Clarke searched through the cupboards and pulled out a teakettle along with a bag of herbs she didn't recognize. "Drink your milk, and I'll make a tea that should help, as well."

"That's not necessary. You're probably tired from your night out, and this should help." She raised her glass, taking a slow sip of the hot liquid to prove her point.

He scoffed. "I went back to the office to work on the figures for the Bath hotel, hardly a wild evening. Besides, I'm not going to leave you down here to suffer alone. Especially when I have a potential solution." Clarke shook out a pile of the herbs into his palm and held it out to her. The familiar scent of citrusy lemon swathed her in comfort—it was the same fragrance that surrounded Clarke whenever he came near. "This is lemongrass from India. I learned about its healing properties years ago. It's helped my mother immensely while calming my own galloping thoughts from time to time. She drinks several cups a day, as do I. I even keep a pocketful handy to chew when tea's not readily available."

Rubbing a pinch of the herb between her fingers, Iris inspected it, brought it to her nose for another sniff, as Clarke focused on brewing a pot of the lemongrass. Perhaps she should worry over seeming weak—enforcing his inaccurate view of her—but she rather adored having him care for her.

"Here. Tell me how you feel after drinking this." A teacup appeared in front of her, and Clarke removed the empty milk glass she'd already finished.

Tentatively, Iris cradled the warm cup and blew across the top, ripples of the tawny-colored liquid dashing against the sides. It smelled delightful. She sipped, then swallowed, considering the unique taste. "It's quite good. You've a talent for domesticity, I see—tea-brewing master," she teased.

"I boiled water, hardly the work of a professional. But I'm glad you like it. Mum will be happy to hear someone else has discovered the benefits of lemongrass tea, too. She swears by the stuff now."

Taking another drink, Iris hummed in relief, the aching in her body beginning to dull from the effects of her two nightcaps. "Your mother is wonderful. Her enthusiasm for stories and learning about the peerage reminds me a little of Hazel. She loves fairytales and happy endings."

"And you don't?" He grinned, softening the question. "Don't think I haven't noticed the stack of novels propped on your vanity. Where most women keep their beauty accoutrements, you've relegated reading material. Though I shouldn't be surprised since you have no need for extra frills. You're exquisite as you are—no additions necessary."

Blushing at the outrageous compliment, Iris ducked her head to avoid his admiring gaze. When he spoke so freely about his appreciation of her attributes, bashfulness rose to the forefront, along with a large sampling of optimism that he'd act upon said appreciation sooner rather than later.

Patience. He'll come around.

"Thank you... And I like to think I'm a tad more grounded than Hazel. Hopefully, you'll agree once you get to know her better. You're still planning on joining me in Hampshire to celebrate the release of her book, correct?" Hazel had written to notify them of her American publisher's acceptance of a second manuscript, along with the impending release of her first book. Apparently, a package of books had arrived commemorating the accomplishment, and she wanted the entire family to gather in celebration of everyone's recent blessings—from her book to baby Benjamin to Iris's wedding.

"I wouldn't miss it. It'll be good to escape Town for a while."

She silently agreed.

"Oh, and your mother is invited, of course. She's part of our family and shouldn't miss out on the festivities if she's feeling well enough to travel." Iris thought her sisters would quite enjoy meeting the elder Mrs. Calloway, and Owen's mother, the dowager countess, could have someone her own age to discuss grandchildren with.

"I will let her know, but I doubt she'll be able to come. Travel for any length of time tends to exhaust her fairly quickly." Clarke pushed back from the table and placed Iris's empty teacup in the sink, covering a yawn with his arm. "If you're feeling better, sleep is calling my name and yours, too, I'd wager. Shall we retire for the evening?"

"Yes, my body's decided to settle down thanks to our combined efforts. Next time, I might try the tea alone to observe its effects."

"And if it loses its effectiveness, we'll find something else to help. There's no need for you to suffer; we have modern medicine for a reason." They ambled upstairs, arms linked, until Iris's room stood before them.

How I wish we were both retiring to the same place.

"It's not always so terrible, and not nearly as debilitating as the ailments plaguing patients at St. Mary's. But I'm grateful for every bit of relief. Thank you again." An air of anticipation bloomed between them as Iris gently swayed towards Clarke, wordlessly pleading for more from him.

He towered above Iris, his shadow fully enveloping her until his head lowered, and an achingly tender kiss skimmed her forehead before grazing her waiting lips. Soothing. Cherishing. It wasn't meant to incite passion, but rather extend peace and caring—to tell her without words how he felt.

The knowledge slipped deep in her heart, filling old cracks, patching over past scars. Their marriage wasn't a love match, but her soul recognized that they could become one.

And it was enough.

For now.

CHAPTER FIFTEEN

Returning from a trip to retrieve a special gift for Iris, Clarke entered his office at the Grand Markham to find Porter tossing a paperweight from his desk between his hands. "What are you doing here?" They hadn't spoken since the dinner party due to Porter's departure for Manchester to oversee their other hotel, the St. James.

"I've come to check on you after the incident with Johnson. Have you seen him?"

"Hell, no. And he better keep it that way. I have enough trouble keeping tabs on Linton without needing to add Johnson to the list." Soon after learning of Linton's debt to his former friend, he hired a man to tail the marquess and report his comings and goings. Already a list of names and amounts owed sat in a drawer of his desk, a compilation of Linton's spending spree throughout London.

Yet somehow the man avoided coming to him for funds.

It couldn't be long now before he crawled out from the gutters of gambling hells asking for financial aid. The question remained whether Clarke would give it. *Don't kid yourself.* He would pay the debts, if only to ensure Iris's happiness. She didn't need more evidence of how much of a lout her father was—the marquess did quite well proving that on his own.

What a difference between her meeting Mum and the marquess.

Iris fit perfectly with his mother as they chatted about books and running a household. His mum clearly adored her after one meeting, whereas Linton still hadn't had dinner alone with them in their own home. Iris had been kind, like he'd expected, and he feared his concern over loving two frail women in his life was coming true. Because it was getting harder and harder to resist his wife's pull.

"Tailing the lord?" Porter plopped into the leather chair across from Clarke's desk, rolling the glass orb over his pant leg. Thankful for the interruption to the turn of his thoughts, he nodded.

"Yes, because he's a damn child who can't comprehend a simple concept: if you're a terrible loser, quit playing the game." Setting Iris's gift in a lower drawer away from prying eyes, Clarke watched his friend trying to balance the paperweight on his knee. "Are you going to play with that all day, or does your visit have an actual purpose?"

"I told you, I wanted to see how you were doing. Johnson's still got his dander up over the ordeal, though I fully support your actions. He's had a punch to the gut coming for a long time now, only surprised it took you so long. How'd the wife take the display of violence?"

Very well.

Iris had been surprisingly eager for his attentions in the carriage ride home, and to have her small hands grasp his cock, milking him to completion... He'd become undone.

They were lucky they'd arrived home when they did, free to put distance between them, because another moment sequestered in close quarters would've broken Clarke's resolve. He was sure of it. Which is why he'd decided to buy the gift he did today.

With his control dissolving by the day, a fresh course of action needed to be taken. Obviously, they couldn't continue as they have been—stealing kisses and brief intimate moments, rather than lingering in bed, consummating their marriage completely. So, he'd devised a solution. One he really should have thought of weeks ago considering his sexual expertise, but Clarke could only blame his blinding obsession for Iris that clouded rational judgment.

"She was understanding. You've met her; she doesn't have a cross bone in her body." Foot tapping the bottom drawer of his desk, he contemplated how to present his gift. It had never been an issue in prior liaisons, but this was his *wife*. Sensitivity and tact were needed.

"You lucked out with her, despite your early misgivings. She ended up being stronger than you thought, hmm?" Porter replaced the paperweight where it belonged and stood, straightening his jacket.

"I won't deny my good fortune." A flicker of movement caught his eye, and Clarke saw the man he'd hired to watch Linton hanging about the doorway. "If you'll excuse me, I have a personal matter to attend to. Perhaps we can meet at Martin's later tonight?"

Spying their visitor, Porter agreed and left the office, leaving the two men alone.

Harris Childress came highly recommended from a contact in the police force, and so far, Clarke hadn't been disappointed by the detective's work ethic or information gathered. Short with nondescript features, he blended into his surroundings, making the freelance reconnaissance jobs he took on an easy moneymaking venture.

"Who's he fucked over this time?" Clarke asked, frustration with the marquess welling in his chest. Could the man not stay out of trouble for the length of a fucking day?

"Beckman, sir. Saw his lordship leaving the den late this morning. By the looks of his appearance, it didn't go so well inside."

"Goddammit."

Childress shrugged his thin shoulders. "Beckman's a bad one, that's for sure. Don't know why a marquess would want to get mixed up with that lot."

"Because he's a damn idiot, that's why." And he's risking hurting Iris if Linton managed to get himself killed by a gang leader. "I'll talk with Linton. In the meantime, continue following him. I appreciate your thoroughness."

Tipping his hat, Childress exited, and Clarke withdrew a blank piece of stationary, penning a pointed warning to Linton to not test his generosity. To have a care for his daughter rather than wasting time and money gambling. He doubted the missive would have much effect, but it made him feel marginally better releasing the flood of reprimands he wanted to shout at the man.

Foolish old man.

Why couldn't Linton see the gem he had in Iris instead of avoiding her like she housed the goddamn plague?

CHAPTER SIXTEEN

After discovering Linton absent from his home and the house in tidy condition, Iris debated her options for the afternoon. She'd hoped to catch her father in a moment of leisure, determined to be more forthright in her desire to know him better, but once again, she was thwarted.

"Where to next, my lady?"

"Baywater, please," she announced, smoothing her skirts once seated inside her carriage. "I wish to visit with my mother-in-law." Surely, Mrs. Calloway—Pru—would be available. *As long as she's not indisposed with a flare up of her angina.*

Iris wondered if it was a mistake to call on the woman without Clarke, but a dose of motherly affection sounded lovely. She'd been without the love of true parents for a while since Mama and Papa died in an accident years ago. The wave of grief had waned, cropping up at odd times rather than remaining a constant companion. However, with the appearance of Linton and Pru in her life, she found herself reminiscing and longing for her adoptive parents more than ever.

The marquess and Clarke's mother were opposite ends of the spectrum for parental love, and a part of her wished they'd fall on the same side. It would certainly ease the turmoil lurching about in her stomach. If they were both distant, then the guilt she felt about gaining another set of parents would be rendered moot. If they were both loving, then she could chalk it up to a blessing from Mama and Papa.

This either/or situation, though...

It filled her with guilt and shame and indecision.

Pitted Pru against Linton, however hard she tried not to compare them, and Linton kept coming out the loser. Which made her feel terrible all over again.

"Here we are, my lady. Baywater." Jimmy offered a hand to help her down to the street, effectively distracting her from the dilemma spinning around in her head.

"Thank you. I'm not sure how long I'll be. Mrs. Calloway may not feel well enough for visitors, so it could be very brief."

The coachman nodded before rounding the carriage to pet the horses, leaving Iris to knock on the heavy oak front door. Maude promptly answered, her eyes widening at Iris's presence, though she swiftly ushered her inside.

"We weren't expecting anyone, my lady. This will be a treat for the missus."

"You're sure it's fine? I don't want to overtax Pru."

"Pish posh." The woman in question called from down the hall. Her diminutive form peeked out the doorway, and she raised her arms for a fond embrace. "You're always welcome, dear. Why, you're the daughter I never had!"

Emboldened by the declaration, Iris let Pru pamper her—taking the offered cup of tea, refusing a blanket to ward off a chill. For a moment, she felt like a young girl again, all her troubles washing away under the gentle ministrations of a mother's care.

"I'm happy to see you're well. This was a spur of the moment decision or else I would've written to see how you were feeling before arriving."

"Oh, there's no need for formalities." Pru sank into the same chair she used the last time Iris visited, a mustard-colored piece that looked comfortable and well-loved. "My son would have everyone believe I'm at death's door some days with the way he tiptoes around my health, but I'm made of sterner stuff than my boy thinks. His father was gone at sea most times, which left me to raise a growing boy as best I could alone. And with my bad heart, I couldn't run around with him as much as I'd have liked. I fear it's taken its toll on him. He's always so cautious, as if I'll break from the slightest inconvenience."

Tears formed in the poor woman's amber eyes—the same shade as Clarke's. "Please don't disparage yourself. You've raised a wonderful son. Yes, he can be overprotective, but it's because he loves you so dearly." Clarke's devotion to Pru inspired Iris, gave her hope that she could earn a modicum of the same devotion from him.

"I know... He's a dear boy..." Raising an embroidered hanky to her eyes, Pru dabbed at a few stray tears before balling the fabric in her bony hands with a watery laugh. "Look at me. You arrive, and I start spouting about the past and turning into a watering pot. Tell me, what news have you to share? Any scandals I should know about?"

"As a matter of fact..." Iris had learned quickly on her first visit how fascinated Pru was with high society, so she'd taken it upon herself to actually read the gossip rags to have sordid tales to tell. Losing herself in the ridiculous anecdotes of lords and ladies prancing about town eased some of the heaviness weighing on her heart.

Frivolity had been lacking in her life of late without Hazel around. It was time she fixed that.

Though Iris wished she could avoid the articles published about a certain marquess. He wasn't mentioned nearly as often as the young bucks gallivanting around London, but every now and then there'd be mention of him exiting a gambling hell looking rather piqued or attending a ball and dancing with a woman half his age.

All occasions that punctured Iris's heart when she considered how little time he'd spent in her company. It seemed social events trumped getting to know his daughter, and the knowledge stung.

Coincidentally, Iris found her father outside her home upon returning from her visit with Pru an hour later. As if summoned by her negative thoughts of him.

"Father! What a lovely surprise! What brings you by?"

What are the odds?

Linton smiled indulgently and pulled her into a brief hug. "Can't I want to see my long-lost daughter? We've hardly spent any time together. Besides, I received the note you left during your visit earlier. I apologize for missing you, my dear."

Ah, fairly decent odds when you consider your letter.

Encouraged by this turn of events, pleasure warmed her belly. It was good to see him, especially after her ruminations earlier, and to chat with not one—*but two*—of her newfound parents all in the same day. "Of course, you're welcome whenever you please." Directing her gaze towards the sitting room, she asked, "Shall I ring for tea?"

"An invigorating peppermint, if you please." He took a seat across from her after she rang for Edith, who promptly brought refreshments. Small talk ensued about the weather as Iris learned Linton's preferences—biscuit with treacle, tea with no sugar, a splash of milk.

Once they were settled, she searched for a topic—suddenly at a loss for words, despite yearning for a private moment to talk with him—until a curious aspect of her father's past popped into her head. "If you don't mind my asking, what was your wife like? Were you terribly in love? You met her after my mother, correct?" Iris imagined two young lovers destined for happily-ever-after before disease wrecked the dream.

"Oh, Lizzy? Uh, yes, we wed a year after my... time with your mother." Linton coughed, then scratched his ear. "Nice girl. The second daughter of Lord Otto. We liked each other well enough."

Not the glowing soliloquy she expected. But perhaps it required more trust between them before he fully opened up. She could be patient. Toying with a crumb on the lace tablecloth covering the cart of treats, Iris again sought an interesting subject—one they could both elaborate on.

"How about Martha Kent, my biological mother? Can you share anything about her?" All she really knew was that the woman was flighty and held no qualms over abandoning her baby. Not the most glowing of traits.

"Martha was beautiful like you. But it didn't surprise me when she ran off. She always fidgeted, always sought diversion. Frankly, it doesn't shock me that she left you with her sister, either. Martha was a fun girl, but not a very responsible one."

Confirmation of her mother's less-than-perfect characteristics wasn't exactly what Iris was looking for, but it was a start.

Preparing to ask for more details, the clock struck two times in the background to interrupt her, and Linton glanced at the wooden tower to his right. "I know my visit was unexpected, but there's a rather important favor I must beg of you."

"Oh?"

"I hate to even ask. You've already done so much..." His eyes softened as they met her questioning ones. "But I'm in another bind. You see, a friend of mine owed me for a horse I sold him a few months ago. He promised to pay me the complete sum after a particular business deal was finalized. However, he's reneged on the deal, and now I'm left floundering for cash."

Her shoulders deflated, a sinking feeling filling her veins. "And you'd like me to loan you the money?" By this point, Iris realized her father probably never intended to pay her back—these exchanges of her jewelry to cover his debts only seemed to increase the frequency with which he requested aid—however, a loan allowed them both to pretend. To put a shiny veneer over an otherwise ugly habit.

"If it's not too much trouble." Linton's apologetic expression tugged at her heartstrings, and she nodded, setting her teacup aside.

No trouble at all...

Forcing a smile, Iris asked him to wait while she retrieved a jewelry set from her room. Surely the proceeds from selling the rubied pieces would be enough to cover whatever costs he incurred—debts from gambling, most likely, the gossip articles sprouting to mind. She hated doubting her father's word, but his story lacked the ring of honesty that the paper had.

If only I felt comfortable questioning him further.

But she didn't want to upset him. He could very well be telling the truth, while she imagined nefarious scenarios after living with Hazel and her stories for so long. Sighing, Iris hurried back downstairs with the bounty in hand. "Here you go. I pray it's enough."

Linton snatched the velvet bag and peeked inside. "Oh, yes. This will be plenty. Thank you, my dear. Now, I must be going, but I've enjoyed our chat today. I'm grateful to have you for a daughter."

Without a backward glance, he strode to the door, a little taller than when he'd entered a quarter hour earlier, and Iris sank into the blue settee once again.

He hadn't wanted to see Iris for herself. He'd visited because he needed something from her.

Don't be uncharitable.

But it was impossible to believe he would've come if there hadn't been a financial motive, despite the note she left about her visit.

What else could she have offered him, anyway? Her conversation wasn't worth much with her limited knowledge of London or any other topic Linton may find interesting. She demonstrated that in spades with the awkward silences that fell between them.

"Was that Linton I saw leaving? What did he want?" Clarke entered the room with long strides, gaze flying to her position on the settee.

"Oh, we had tea together. Nothing special," she lied. The fib itched at her sense of honesty but informing her husband of Linton's need for money again wasn't exactly in her plan to win his love. She wanted to create a path of least resistance, which meant no troubling family issues.

Clarke's brows scrunched at his forehead as if he meant to question her further, so she pasted on a smile and beat him to the punch. "How was your day? It's rather early for you to be home already, isn't it?"

Granted, he kept flexible hours with his many ventures—ventures she didn't know much about except for the three hotels he co-owned with Porter—but he usually didn't return home until right before supper commenced.

"Shall I leave and return later?"

"Don't be ridiculous. Why don't we go to the bookshop? We haven't strolled about town very much, and perhaps we'll find Hazel's book already gracing their shelves." Fresh air might clear her head, too.

Clarke studied her for another minute before agreeing. "If that's what you want, then that's what we'll do. My lady?" He swept a gallant arm out, and Iris placed her hand upon it, letting her husband escort her away from the lingering sense of disappointment Linton left behind in the parlor.

"Tell me about your childhood." Iris recalled the stories Pru shared during their visit, but she wanted to hear Clarke's side of things. How he viewed his upbringing.

They ambled down the sidewalk, a slight breeze ruffling their hair, as he contemplated her request. "Nothing much to tell. My father was away at sea for long stretches, and I helped my grandfather in the butcher's shop when I wasn't caring for my mother. I knew love. Wasn't mistreated. By all accounts, it was idyllic if one ignored our location near the docks."

"What about friends? Don't say you spent the majority of your youth working for your grandfather." Though it wasn't unheard of for children to aid their families, Iris prayed he had a little respite with boys his own age.

Clarke shrugged. "Sure, I got into mischief with a group of boys, but none of those friendships lasted long. We all took different paths, especially once my mother had me dedicate so much time to my education. What about you? I've heard about the antics of the Taylor sisters, but no other names have been mentioned."

"That's because Caraway, Hazel, and Lily were my closest confidantes. The four of us stuck together, along with Owen. We never felt the need to expand past our circle. We were friendly with the village children, but like you, nothing serious ever developed. I think that's why I've struggled a bit here," she admitted.

"Have you?" Concern immediately cropped into his tone. "I had no idea... How can I help you?"

Sweet man.

"I'm afraid you can't. Unless we attend more social gatherings, although large group settings tend to overwhelm me. And as silly as it sounds, I don't have much practice making friends. My life kind of came with them already installed since I have sisters." Her one attempt to befriend Mrs. Franklin and the cook had been an abysmal failure—not that the women weren't kind, but there was a boundary of employer and employee that she couldn't cross.

"Have more faith in yourself, sprite," Clarke chastised as the bookshop came into view. "Anyone would be lucky to call you friend, and you naturally exude a welcoming aura to others. If no one's taken the time to get to know you better, then that's their mistake. At our next social event, I'll make sure we visit with every young woman you might have a commonality with. But don't forget about your poor lonely husband when you're hosting breakfasts and charity galas with your new circle of friends."

Iris laughed at the absurd prediction. She could never forget *him*. He lived deeply ensconced in her mind, body, and soul.

"Thank you for the vote of confidence. Now, shall we search for Hazel's book?" They reached the bookshop, and she scanned the display of books in the window.

"If they don't own it, we'll request it. Praise her work until they realize what a disaster it is to not shelf the title."

"Superb plan!" Like two matchmaking mamas in cahoots, Iris and Clarke entered the shop with twin smiles.

And she couldn't help but fall a little more in love with her kind and handsome husband.

CHAPTER SEVENTEEN

Nothing compared to a leisurely ride through the countryside.

Fields of green waved cheerful greetings while livestock ambled through the thick foliage, unruffled by the passage of humble wagons or extravagant carriages. For Iris, this homecoming was a much-needed respite from the hubbub of London with its industrialized buildings and commerce—and the familial problems that plagued her.

Here in Shoreham, she'd have her sisters and Owen and could lose herself in their happy lives. Linton wouldn't appear asking for more money. Clarke and she would be able to spend quality time together in a setting more conducive to intimate conversations. It was a recipe for the ideal holiday.

A high-pitched squeal interrupted the peaceful silence of the carriage as they stopped in front of the Trent home, and Iris smiled at the picture her rambunctious nephew made wiggling in his mother's arms. Her entire family awaited their arrival on the drive rather than lounging about inside. Even the dowager had decided to join the fray, a frilly parasol held aloft to deflect the sun's brilliant rays, though signs of an impending storm edged the eastern sky.

"Someone's eager to see his Aunt Iris." Lily traipsed forward as little Benjamin's chubby arms lurched towards Iris, who'd burst from the carriage without a second thought for propriety.

"And I'm just as keen to see him." Catching the boy as he practically leapt from Lily's arms in excitement, Iris held him in a secure embrace and cooed. "Hello, little cherub. Have you been a good boy while I've been gone?"

"Depends on your definition of good." Owen ruffled the wisps of russet hair on Benjamin's head before dropping an affection kiss to Iris's temple. "Welcome home. We've missed having the full set of Garden Girls in Shoreham."

"Garden Girls?" Clarke's query reminded Iris that she hadn't come alone—so lost in her family, she'd completely abandoned him in the carriage.

Red with contrition, Iris explained, "That's his nickname for us. Caraway, Iris, Lily, and Hazel. Our names are forms of flora, thanks to our parents' love of botany."

"He mostly uses the moniker to tease us mercilessly." Cara neared and wrapped an arm around Iris's waist. "How was the train ride? Everything run smoothly?"

The family moved indoors as Iris and Clarke fielded questions about their journey and London, while refreshments were dispersed by a bevy of servants impeccably dressed in black and white. Lemon and berry tarts, buttery biscuits, and hot tea filled the room with an aroma of mouthwatering scents, and everyone happily relaxed after the various journeys taken to arrive in Hampshire.

Eventually, someone called for Hazel's book to be brought in, eliciting several exclamations from Iris as she flipped through the children's story. "What a marvelous feat you've accomplished! Mama and Papa would be so proud to see your words and illustrations printed for the world to read. Oh, and your publisher should be receiving an order from Barnaby Books after the way Clarke and I pushed for them to purchase your story." She shared a satisfied grin with Clarke after mentioning their afternoon together the week prior.

Colorful animals graced each page of the book along with an effervescent fairy who bore a remarkable resemblance to Iris.

"Thank you... And you think so? About Mama and Papa being proud?" Hazel nervously asked, and Iris watched as Jonathan, Hazel's husband, draped an arm over her shoulders, cuddling her close. The brazen display of affection ignited a flicker of envy inside her belly. She wished her relationship with Clarke could be equally open and loving—not that she doubted they were on the right path, but it was taking longer than she'd like.

"I do, and I'm flattered that I served as inspiration, too." Iris presented the book side by side with her face, showcasing the uncanny likeness between her and its main character.

"A sprite in fiction and reality," Clarke murmured next to her.

"Better you than me." Lily shook her head good-naturedly and Cara seconded the opinion. Both sisters, the more practical of the four women, tolerating fairytales rather than believing in them as fully as Iris and Hazel.

"I'm impressed that you found time to author a book while teaching and working with Jonathan at the boarding house. Oh, and raising young Peter." The dowager countess drawled from her place at the edge of the room. Like a mother hen with her chicks, she watched over them, basking in the light of children and grandchildren.

"It wasn't easy."

"And now we have another venture to occupy our time..." Hazel tacked on to Jonathan's comment. They shared a conspiratorial look before glancing towards Owen who shrugged, then nodded as if in permission.

"We've decided to build a textile factory in Manchester," Jonathan said. "Through the tenants at the boarding house and my own experiences, it's clear a modern way of doing things is needed. A factory that prioritizes employees' safety and health. Owen and I have discussed it at length, and together with another mill owner in Manchester, we'll build such a place."

"I'd be interested in hearing more about this venture," Clarke added. "Possibly investing if you need any more capital."

Iris whipped her head towards her husband—wincing in pain from the grip Benjamin had on her hair tightening—and marveled at his casual offer of aid. She knew he was generous. Towards her, his mother, and even Linton, but Jonathan and Owen were practically strangers, despite being relations through marriage. He didn't need to extend anything more than congratulations and good wishes.

The fact that he chose to go beyond what was necessary to be polite sent a thrill of adoration quivering down her spine.

"Shall we put Benjamin down for a nap, while the men discuss business? Frankly, I've heard all I care to about profit margins and construction costs. I'd much rather chat with my sisters in a factory-free zone." Lily hopped to her feet and gathered her fretful son from Iris as the Garden Girls adjourned from the drawing room, along with the dowager trailing behind to rest in her own chambers.

Iris felt a degree of guilt for leaving Clarke behind, but he was a capable man. He could handle himself with her brothers-in-law.

"Now that we're alone. How are you, Iris? How's married life? Any babes on the horizon?" Hazel's gaze dropped to her stomach, and Iris shook her head.

"Not as yet." *And not any time soon, considering my husband and I haven't consummated our marriage.* Perhaps this holiday would be the perfect opportunity to change that. With her family boosting her confidence, Iris could seduce Clarke... or at least try. She knew he wasn't immune to her, but his steely resolve was a firm barrier to overcome. "Besides..." Diverting the topic to someone else whilst concocting a plan of seduction for later, Iris said, "It's Cara we should concern ourselves with. Marriage trumps forthcoming children, for the moment, because I want to see us all happily wed."

"Perhaps I enjoy being a spinster." The nonchalant rebuttal from Caraway convinced no one. Out of the four sisters, as the eldest, she was the one most made for marriage and family with her cool head and responsible nature. It was a shame she hadn't found love yet.

"You know that's not true," Hazel mumbled as if only for Cara's ears. Again, Iris noticed a silent discussion wage between their clashing gazes—the same look she'd noticed on her wedding day—and wondered what they knew that Lily and she did not.

Perhaps it's about Miles Brandon.

It was no secret that Caraway held a secret tendre for Owen's old friend, though she'd never admit it aloud. But maybe she'd finally shared something of her feelings with Hazel.

"Of course, it's not," Lily interjected quietly, laying Benjamin down in his bassinet. "Let's make a list of potential suitors; that's the first step."

"Lord save me." Cara covered her face in exasperation and flopped into a rocking chair as everyone began citing names of eligible bachelors amid giggles and dreamy sighs.

Yes, it was good to be home.

CHAPTER EIGHTEEN

Marrying an illegitimate lady was meant to be a snub to Society's standards on class, yet somehow Clarke gained an earl and countess as in-laws who upended his views on nobility. Perhaps he'd spent too much time fleecing lords at Martin's. Perhaps he'd given Linton and his ilk too much power over his thoughts. Because the Earl and Countess of Trent—*please call me Lily*—weren't uppity and self-righteous, nor did they act as if Clarke didn't belong due to his parentage.

His first clue that they were a different sort of family was an earl marrying a simple country girl.

The second was the countess toting the baby around, no nursemaid in sight.

Take away the sumptuous surroundings and fine clothing, and they could be any one of the families who'd neighbored his childhood home. For once, he regretted the lack of his mother's presence at a noble affair because this wouldn't have disabused her of the lofty visions she held of Society, it would've cemented them as living fairytale lives.

"How's life with Lord Linton as an in-law?" Trent asked, sinking a striped ball into a corner pocket as the men had migrated to a billiards room down the hall.

"Tolerable."

Trent and Travers laughed, reading between the lines of his sardonic tone. The next shot flew wide, and Travers rounded the table while Clarke looked on from his position against the wall. Of a similar age, though he held a few extra years on the younger men, they seemed intelligent types, hardworking—the kind of men he'd befriend naturally if their wives hadn't brought them together.

"I regret not telling Iris sooner about Linton. We may have avoided a barrel of trouble, otherwise." A true enough assessment, but Clarke didn't like the idea of not having Iris as his wife. *Selfish, really.* She'd be better off without Linton or him mucking about in her life.

At least you don't have to worry about Linton here.

Hopefully, Iris could enjoy a taste of her real family, the ones who loved her unconditionally, and stop feeling the need to bring the marquess up to snuff. Because Clarke hated witnessing her disappointment after every lackluster interaction with her biological father.

"I'm trying to point him down the straight and narrow, but he refuses to heed warnings. I've resorted to placing a tail on him, so I'm aware when he gets into trouble," he confided, willing to build a real friendship with the men by disclosing a fact he hadn't even told Iris. Clarke doubted she'd take it well, and he didn't want her to worry, regardless. If an issue arose, he planned on dealing with it before it ever touched his wife.

Travers and Trent's twin expressions of surprise and gratitude made him uncomfortable. Crossing his ankles, he fidgeted with his sleeve. He wanted to be esteemed by them, but make no mistake—he wasn't a *good* man. At his core, he was a scoundrel, even if he did exhibit respectable qualities every now and then.

"Well, if you require assistance wrangling the man, don't hesitate to send word. I'll catch the earliest train to London."

"As will I," Travers confirmed, sinking the last ball to win the game. Trent held out his cue, and Clarke took the wooden stick, likening it to a peace offering of sorts. While the men hadn't been outwardly rude, they'd remained guarded, testing Clarke. But it looked like he may have finally passed their assessment with his roundabout way of protecting Iris.

Chalking his cue, Clarke nodded in gratitude for their willingness to provide help with his father-in-law before teasing, "I hope you're ready to lose." With the challenge declared, conversation lightened to ruthlessly ribbing each other, and the afternoon continued in friendly competition—the beginning of brotherly bonding that Clarke found oddly endearing.

YOU CAN DO THIS. YOU'VE lasted this long.

Clarke assumed Iris and he would have separate bedrooms at the Trent home. Why? He couldn't rightly say, but one thing was certain: he'd assumed wrong.

Because here he stood in their room hours later with one massive bed dominating the center while his wife looked delectable in a robin's egg blue peignoir meant for seduction rather than sleeping.

Bloody hell.

"What's this, sprite?" he asked cautiously. Iris hadn't pushed him too hard in this area lately, seemingly content with waiting for him to change his mind. However, if she chose to press her advantage—use the knowledge of Clarke's attraction to her—then he was well and truly finished.

"I want us to... make love." The words may have stumbled out, but they rang clear in the room. "I care for you, and you hold a measure of affection for me. There's no reason for a continued distance between us."

Clarke searched for a compelling reason to refuse her and found none. *You bought her gift for a purpose.* Between work and travel, he hadn't broached the topic yet, the timing always seeming off. But now would be as good a time as any, he supposed.

Men fuck their wives all the time, and they survive.

Even his fragile mother had survived his birth. Surely, sex wasn't as traumatic as childbirth.

And with his gift, he'd ease Iris's introduction to his carnal appetites. "You're right. We've reached the end of this particular path, and it's time to walk a new one. Which is why I got you something. I debated bringing it with me, but clearly, my gut instinct proved correct." Rifling through his unpacked trunk of belongings, Clarke located the ornate jewelry box and awkwardly presented it to Iris.

"I don't need more jewelry as thoughtful as it is." She tried to return the box, but he shifted back to sit on the edge of the bed.

"It's not jewelry. Open it up, and I'll explain."

Confusion twisted her mouth and lines of doubt striped her forehead—he almost wondered if she'd fight him in a contest of wills—but in the end, Iris unlatched the box and stared speechlessly at its contents.

"Do you know what that is? What it's for?"

Iris picked up the wooden object before setting aside its packaging. "Please tell me it's not meant for what I think it is."

"There's no need to be afraid. It's a dildo, an item intended to aid us in consummation." Clasping his hands between his knees, he watched her study the phallus with caution. "You know my concerns about our body differences. About me hurting you. This will allow me to gently prepare you for when I eventually take you. It's smaller than my cock, so it shouldn't pain you as much."

Thunder roared outside, announcing the arrival of a storm before the sound of torrential rain splattered against the window. Iris's silence lengthened, became a rope around his neck that threatened to choke him with its weight.

What is she thinking?

"You must be joking." Silver lightning flared to life in Iris's normally serene gaze, and Clarke tensed as she returned the wooden toy to its casing before slamming the top shut. Casting the high-quality dildo aside as if he hadn't labored over which size and shape would work best for her. "I don't want a... a... *facsimile* of you. I want you!"

Clarke stalked forward—his own anger stoked by her rejection of a compromise. He was giving her what he could, what she could take. Why didn't she understand he was doing this to protect her? "You want me, do you? Want a feral husband whose only concern is spending in your cunt without a care for your wellbeing?"

Iris held her ground, refusing to budge despite his aggressive advance.

Stubborn little sprite.

"Yes. If that's what it'll take, then that's what I want."

He scoffed, pacing in front of her. "You don't know what you want. You can't. *I'm* the one with actual experience. *I'm* the one who knows what's best."

"Don't talk to me as if I'm a child. I'm a grown woman."

"Oh, I know what you are. You're tiny and fragile and will bruise the moment my hands drag you over my cock." *Snap. Snap. Snap.* His bounds were unraveling under her obstinacy. She kept poking and prodding, daring him to prove her wrong. *If you crack, you could hurt her.*

"I may bruise. But I won't break. A misconception you cling to as if it were one of the Ten Commandments. Thou shall not fuck wives no taller than a cornstalk. Do you hear how outlandish it sounds?" Iris crossed her arms over her heaving chest, her breathing labored with indignant fury.

That's it. She cursed. His sweet little sprite spouting filthy epithets was the last straw.

"My cock will stretch your virgin cunt until you cry, begging me to retreat. But by then it'll be too late. I'll know the snug squeeze of your pussy milking me, the tight heat that only belongs to me. You think I'll hear your pleas and leave? You think I won't keep rutting inside you like a fucking beast? Forcing you to accept every drop of my seed, so you're bellyful before the year ends?"

"You think to scare me, but I'm not afraid. I'm not a tender seedling sprouting from the earth for the first time. Let me prove my strength to you," she implored, some of the anger leaving her eyes. "We can even use your gift. It was thoughtful, and I'm grateful for your forethought... I just..." A beleaguered sigh fell from her lips. "I'm just tired of this distance between us. Even when it seems we grow closer by leaps and bounds, there's still this chasm to overcome."

"It's there for a reason. Because I care too damn much for you," he growled. "You've made me into a ravening beast when it comes to fucking you—hell, to even being near you. You have no idea the control I've exerted these past weeks, but you *will* see the dam broken tonight." He clamped her hips in a brutal grip of ownership. "Because that's what you want, and I can't deny you a damn thing. So, get on your hands and knees, sprite. *Now.*"

CHAPTER NINETEEN

Perhaps she shouldn't be so eager to comply with his demand.

Especially since he'd concocted a plan of taking her virginity with a wooden sex toy! Irritation ran through her veins at the notion, as if Iris would prefer a mockery of the real thing. But passion—whether from frustration or desire—ran hot and too close together, so she swiftly lowered to the carpeted floor of their chamber.

If this is how he wants to proceed, then so be it. At least we're getting somewhere.

Besides, the toy *had* intrigued her. It was just the idea of it being a replacement for Clarke that raised her ire. Raising the gossamer skirt of the seductive nightgown she'd donned, Iris wiggled her bottom at her husband, taunting him.

"You're looking for trouble tonight, aren't you, sprite? Or else you wouldn't be waving your ass about the air, daring me to commit all sorts of filthy acts upon your innocent little body."

"I'd settle for one filthy act first," she said, provoking him with a boldness that thus far had been hidden behind layers of shy reserve. But he'd pushed her past the limits of propriety. They'd been married for several months with nary a shared bed between them, and Iris couldn't stomach it anymore.

Clarke's heat settled over her back, forcing her upper body flush against the floor while her hips arched upward to meet his groin. "Careful what you wish for," he gritted, one hand circling her neck to ensure she remained in this vulnerable position. Iris's breath stuttered at the lack of freedom—and the unusual spark of need it elicited in her core.

A jolt of lightning lit the room, thunder cracking overhead, and Clarke took the opportunity to smack her bottom, the sound masked by nature's boom. "That's for challenging me." Two fingers burrowed between her thighs, sliding deep into her pussy without preamble. "And this is for disregarding my gift to you. You're going to pay for that with this cunt. Because trust me, wife, you want me to fuck you with whatever toy I choose."

Yes, I believe I do.

As long as he didn't use them as a substitute for himself, then Iris found it thrilling to explore a world of sensuality and sex previously closed to her.

His lips skimmed her exposed back and shoulders, nipping periodically, until his teeth tugged on her earlobe. "Are you ready, sprite?" The slick retreat of his fingers was replaced by the cool head of the dildo poised at her opening. "Because my walls are down. The mask is off. You want me? This is it." He nudged further in. "A scoundrel of a man who bought you for his own pleasure. An obsessed beast desperate to consume you. You're mine, Iris. Say it."

Her body stretched to accept his intrusion—her mind going blank, overwhelmed by every word and touch. But her heart expanded, fluttering wildly about her chest as she gave him what he wanted, what she needed. To belong. To be his.

"I'm yours, Clarke. Yours alone."

"Good girl," he praised, and she felt his body shift until his tongue laved her stretched opening, causing her to jolt in surprise. His fingers returned to the tingling bud atop her sex as he drew circles around it, his tongue lapping the sensitive spot before easing the entry of the wooden toy with wet licks. Eventually the dildo rested entirely within her clenching walls, and Clarke hummed in approval, gently maneuvering the hard phallus to ready her for his own possession.

"Is this what you needed?" he moved to whisper in her ear, punctuating the words with a push of the toy. "Is this what you envisioned when you thought of me fucking this sweet cunt?"

Clarke removed the dildo before she could answer. Then, a powerful thrust of his hips buried his cock to the hilt—a hotter thickness that exceed the length and girth of the wooden phallus. Their bodies were flush together, and a muffled cry caught in her throat. Hot. Cold. Burning in extremes. The scratchy carpet beneath her cheek, her feral husband blanketing her from above.

She was spinning like a children's top. Around and round, with no sense of direction. All Iris knew was Clarke and his possession. He'd feared hurting her with his size, but the slight ache quickly morphed into the need for more. He worried about marking her, yet the sting of teeth on her skin only invigorated her.

Suddenly, Clarke shifted, leaving her empty and chilled. "No, don't go," she begged, worried he'd bring the dildo back instead, and her hands dug into the floor as she tried to chase his withdrawal.

"I'm not leaving you, sprite. I only need to sate my thirst." His meaning became clear when the flick of his tongue edged along her slick folds. "Your thighs are sticky with your cream, distracting me—beseeching me to not let it go to waste. I can't keep my mouth off you and this sweet cunt." Mutual groans of satisfaction emanated in the room as Clarke fervently licked at her clitoris... her inner thighs... the needy clasping of her pussy.

It felt dirty. Wicked. His cock had just filled her, and now his tongue charted the same path.

Sinful. Depraved. *Delicious.*

But not enough.

"Please, Clarke... I need your..." Iris trailed off, hoping he understood what she was asking.

"What? What do you need? Say the word."

Panting, her breasts flattened against the floor upon a shallow inhale, the words flew out of her mouth like skylarks racing in the sky. "I need your... cock. I feel empty without you." And she detested the feeling. After so long with his desires carefully held at bay, Iris refused to accept anything less than all of him, all at once.

"As you wish, sprite." His teeth nipped at her clit one last time before the steel length of his cock drove forward, pinning her to the ground, the muscles in her legs yielding to the force of his body as they widened to a point bordering on pain. She wasn't accustomed to such physical activity, but she wouldn't complain.

The pain melded with the pleasure. Heightened it somehow.

And Iris refused to reign in a feral Clarke, who'd finally let go.

The storm outside gentled, rain falling in lazy streams down the windows. Something banged against the glass—*a loose shutter?* —yet the Calloways remained firmly lodged in their own tempest, oblivious to the world around them. Iris forgot they weren't home in London. She forgot Owen and Lily slept down the hall.

And most importantly, worrisome thoughts about Linton disappeared under the onslaught of her husband's lovemaking.

"Christ, you're so perfect for me," Clarke grunted near her ear. "Wet and wanton. A tiny little sprite who takes my cock like you were born to it." The coarse praise sank into her skin, into her soul. Iris wanted to be perfect for him. Wanted him to love her.

"I'm close, sprite. I'm going to pump you full of my seed, then I'm going to watch it drip down your thighs before shoving it back into this tight cunt. You'll remember this night—remember that I own you. It's what you need, isn't it?"

She didn't know if he expected an answer, but she nodded anyway, her cheek chafing along the carpet. With renewed vigor, Clarke's thrusts deepened, hitting a spot inside her that sent a shiver throughout her body until finally it all became too much.

Their argument. His domination. Everything centered in the connection of their bodies, and Iris cried out at the devastating release pouring through her veins. Trembling with fatigue, she collapsed beneath Clarke, a shout of satisfaction preceding the warmth of his own climax bursting forth.

Like he promised, they lay together in a heap on the floor, Clarke occasionally cupping her pussy to keep her full of him until he deemed it safe to rise. Easing Iris into his arms, she burrowed gratefully into his warmth, too sleepy to register much of his movements as he prepared them for bed.

"Are you alright?" The soft question roused her enough to open her eyes to see Clarke's expression lined with concern.

Precious man.

Yawning, Iris tugged on his arm, wordlessly urging him to lie beside her under the heavy mattress covers. "Yes, *finally*. I'm not hurt, nor do I regret what we've done. So, rest easy, husband, and join me." For a moment, he seemed hesitant, but then the bed dipped, and she found herself cocooned in his strong embrace.

The perfect end to their fresh beginning.

MORNING DAWNED MUCH too soon in Iris's estimation. She wanted to laze about bed with Clarke but knew it wouldn't be possible with her sister and their families present. Rolling to her side, she kissed the thick stubble on her husband's cheek before pestering him with more along his neck and chest, eager to wake him and gauge his feelings about last night.

Surely, he must recognize my strength now.

He'd taken her twice more during the night, gentle couplings compared to their first unrestrained joining, but nonetheless pleasurable or masterful. Soreness permeated her muscles, and she discovered a couple of bruises forming on her wrists where he'd held her down, but overall, Iris felt galvanized to take on the day. So they could get to the night and more lovemaking.

"Good morning, sprite. How are you feeling?" Clarke mumbled in a graveled tone, sleep keeping his eyes closed.

"Wonderful. Rejuvenated. Ready to conquer anything my sisters throw at us today."

"Ah, chipper, too, hmm?" A satisfied grin tilted his lips before he finally blinked awake and studied her with fondness. "You're not in any pain after last night?"

Iris stroked his cheek, enjoying the freedom to do so without him pulling away. "No more than I suspect is usual for women after their first time." Clarke brought the palm of her hand to his lips and pressed a kiss to the center.

"And you wouldn't be underestimating the level of soreness for my benefit, would you?" His teeth nipped at the flesh beneath her thumb in warning, and Iris shuddered at the immediate spike of desire it elicited. Unfortunately, they didn't have time to explore further because already the sounds of the house waking for a new day seeped through the walls. Footsteps hurrying by. Muted voices fading in and out.

"No, I would not. Trust me." Iris shuffled higher on his chest until their eyes were level as she asked the question that would determine how the rest of their holiday went. Would they move forward as a true married couple, occupying the same bed and making love? Or would Clarke retreat from her yet again? "Now, it's time for you to be honest. Are we past this concern over our size difference? Past your fear of harming me by accident? Because I would love for us to use this trip to start anew as husband and wife."

Clarke contemplated her words, and she poured all her hope and optimism into their shared gaze—beseeching him to agree. If he didn't, she wasn't sure what else could be done to convince him.

An audible swallow came from him as his chest rose and fell with a heavy sigh. "I would like that, too. I can't admit to feeling no apprehension at all, but last night certainly quelled most of my worries. We'll try things your way and see how it goes. Besides, it would be a bit awkward to ask for a separate room from your sister now."

Exhaling a breath of relief, Iris tapped his nose playfully before rolling off the bed to prepare for breakfast. "Yes, it would, and I bet she'd deny you, anyway. Taylor girls—even former ones—stick together."

"I figured as much..." Clarke scratched the back of his head as he sat up, and she couldn't help but admire her husband's muscular physique. So big and strong. So utterly attractive.

"If you keep eyeing me that way, we won't make it downstairs in time to eat, and I don't think you want your entire family to hear you screaming my name as I fuck that tight cunt into the mattress. Would make for a memorable meal of tea and sausage, though."

Flushing at the image, Iris shook her head at his teasing. "I can't help that I find you immensely handsome..." Clarke hopped to his feet and prowled closer with an unholy light gleaming in his amber eyes. She took a step backward towards the adjoining water closet—which more closely resembled a room with its spacious size. "And I doubt anyone could hear us all the way up here..." She wasn't entirely confident in such an assertion, but Iris quite adored the lustful rumble emanating from her husband's throat.

When her hand reached the water closet doorknob, she ended the mischievous ribbing with a final, "However, you're quite right. We mustn't miss the serving of sausage. It appears I'm suddenly rather famished," before whipping through the doorway and locking Clarke out. He muttered a crude reference to the sausage that had her giggling like a schoolgirl, then Iris waited until she heard him going through his trunks for fresh clothing before seeing to her own morning ablutions.

Humming a jaunty tune, it was as if her body floated on the air, weightless and full of satisfaction. Her decision to seduce Clarke with another gorgeous nightgown had proved fruitful, and now the rest of their visit lay before them with all sorts of romantic possibilities.

Such as boating on the lake that afternoon where Lily tipped Owen overboard, but Clarke glared warningly at anyone who dared think to tip Iris into the cold water.

And the next evening when the entire family almost expired from laughing during a game of charades, her husband's hand finding hers in the melee.

Each day and activity deepened their relationship until the afternoon they were set to go home, and Iris realized she loved him. Loved Clarke Calloway with all of her heart. And while presumptuous and wildly optimistic, she had a feeling that her scoundrel of a husband may be a little in love with her, too.

CHAPTER TWENTY

"You look beautiful, Mum. Is that a new shawl?" Clarke finished pouring their tea and sat back on the settee, studying the lavender silk draping his mother's shoulders. He'd missed her while away in Hampshire. An idyllic holiday after he and Iris finally came to terms with each other—*and how lovely the terms*, he mused—he decided their next trip to the countryside would include her.

Rail cars were outfitted for comfort these days if one spent the right amount of blunt. Which Clarke had in spades, willing to pay whatever exorbitant sum it took to get his mother safely and comfortably to meet Iris's family and relax in air not polluted with industry.

"Yes, Iris brought it by before your visit to Hampshire. Isn't it lovely?" She petted the shimmery material with delight. "Such a good girl. You're fortunate to have her."

The revelation of Iris's visits with his mum momentarily stunned him. Whenever he asked his wife about her day, she never mentioned going to Baywater. And with Linton's household finally righting itself, he'd assumed Iris spent the majority of her time there. It didn't occur to him that she'd want to speak with his mother privately.

And why not? You know she's as kind as they come.

Their trip to Hampshire had only cemented the knowledge.

"She loves you, you know."

Shaken by the assertion, Clarke waded through his shock, searching for solid ground. "What? Has she said something?"

"Not in so many words. But I recognize when a woman's in love. Been there myself with your father." Pausing, she glanced heavenward before meeting his gaze, a glossy sheen clouding her brown eyes. "I know it hasn't been easy being my son. Sometimes I fear my bad health has affected you worse than myself, and I apologize for the strain it's put on you."

"Mum..."

A trembling hand lifted to stop his rebuttal. "No, don't deny it. I've seen the caution lining your expression every time you visit. Witnessed the same restraint around Iris, which I assume is due to our physical similarities. But Iris is a strong young woman. Please don't push her away out of fear because of me." She dabbed at the corner of her eye with a hanky pulled from her sleeve. "I couldn't bear it if my illness prevented your happiness any more than it already has."

Rising from his seated position, Clarke knelt in front of his mother, gathering her delicate hands within his sturdy ones. "My life is my own. Based on my decisions. I love you." He squeezed her hands. "You are not responsible for the decisions I make—good or bad. You are not a burden to me. Caring for you is a privilege. And as far as Iris..." An image of his diminutive wife emerged, only this time he allowed himself to recognize the strength in her small form.

In Hampshire, she'd taken him into her body. She'd borne the marks of his possession yet still asked for more. His mother had the right of it calling Iris a 'strong young woman'. The time they spent together had proven how capable and resilient Iris was. Their lovemaking had only escalated after that first joining as he claimed her during every moment of freedom from her family—in a meadow during a picnic, in the conservatory with the sounds of rain pattering down overhead. But if he were completely honest, his favorite moments were those spent sleeping next to her, hearing her slight snores and brushing wayward wisps of hair off her cheeks.

He simply adored her, plain and simple.

Clearing his throat—too uncomfortable with the direction of such intimate thoughts—he began again, "As far as Iris, I'm trying to be less overbearing in my protection of her. I recognize that you are two different people, and she deserves to be treated as such. Instead of an extension of you and your ailments."

"That's all I ask." Mum patted his cheek fondly before shooing him away with a light push. Drying a stray tear, her lips arranged into a wobbly smile. "Now, tell me of the earl and countess. What was it like on a noble estate?"

Like a dream.

And for once, he didn't secretly scoff at his mother's fascination with the peerage, because the Trents proved there were families worth learning about, worth knowing. Launching into a stream of anecdotes—every one true and endearing—Clarke spoke with a deep affection even he wouldn't have realized he held.

But his mother, who knew him better than any other, rested her head on the cushioned back of her chair and felt immeasurable gratitude for her daughter-in-law and her family.

Her son was in good hands, and it was all a mother could ask for.

IRIS DECIDED TO VISIT Linton while Clarke caught up with Pru after their trip, giving them private time together since she'd arranged to have tea with her mother-in-law the following afternoon. The two of them being dutiful children amused her as they went their separate ways, though she feared her meeting with Linton would drastically differ from the Calloway reunion.

Because she'd come to a tough conclusion in Hampshire.

Her father had a problem, and he needed help.

She could only guess at how he lost such large sums so quickly—gambling the obvious answer, though a small part of her hoped it was just his bad luck with acquaintances—but Iris was determined to intervene to save him from himself. Perhaps without debts or the thrill of a bet hounding him around every corner, Linton would finally deign to spend more than a few minutes in her presence. Perhaps they could talk without the cloud of money hovering over their heads.

Blanketed in her family's love for the past fortnight had forced Iris to realize that their father-daughter relationship paled in comparison, despite the efforts she'd made to be a good daughter—marrying a stranger, attending his friends' dinners, paying his debts. And no matter how fearful it made her to confront Linton, she knew it was necessary.

It may not be as bad I think.

After all, the argument between Clarke and she ended with them consummating their marriage in the most delicious of ways, demolishing the protective cage her husband had placed her in. An uncomfortable conversation with Linton might benefit their relationship, as well.

"Father, how are you doing today?" Iris asked, marching into his study with determination. *At least he looks sober.* Buoyed by the positive start, she settled in a chair across from his desk and waited for his response.

"I'm well, though I wasn't expecting your visit. Did I miss an appointment?" Linton barely spared her a glance over the sheaf of papers in front of him, and her confidence deflated a bit at the dismissal.

"No, but I wanted to see you after being in Hampshire for so long. It's a shame you couldn't join us. Everyone would've loved to have you." A minor fib. Owen and Jonathan *did* want to speak with Linton, but she doubted it would have been a pleasant conversation. Her family wished to learn more about her father than the sparse details she spoke of or the scraps of gossip that made its way to their ears.

"Yes, well, a marquess's duty is never done." He lifted the stack of paperwork in front of him as if they were explanation enough for his absence. However, Iris wondered exactly what his duty entailed, since it didn't seem to include a sustainable way of filling his coffers.

Don't be unkind.

Even if it's true?

"In that case, it sounds like you need a break. Shall I ring for tea? We can chat about your upcoming birthday—I'd love to host a dinner—and another... more sensitive topic."

"Oh? Your husband giving you trouble?" Linton's interest piqued at the notion, and Iris found it disturbing that his mind would immediately lean towards marital problems with undisguised glee like a Society gossip hearing the tastiest morsel of information. Shouldn't concern be his chief emotion if Clarke and she were at odds?

"No, Clarke is a good husband. You chose well." *One mark in his favor.* "It's actually about your... gambling habit?" she ventured, curious to see how he'd respond.

Reclining in his leather seat, Linton steepled his fingers, eyes narrowing. "So, Calloway's been filling your head with nonsense, hmm? Gambling is a natural pastime among men—one your husband partakes in, as well. It's not a dirty *habit.*"

A nauseous rumbling erupted in her stomach at his tone, like she was an annoying insect he dearly wished to bat from existence. *This is why I hate conflict.* Iris didn't like upsetting people. She stayed calm and congenial, didn't stir up trouble. "Clarke and I haven't spoken about this. I'd prefer to keep it between the two of us, where it's been." At least, she assumed Clarke didn't know about Linton's need for cash. He hadn't said anything to her about paying off more debts.

But would he?

Choosing to focus on one issue at a time, Iris continued, "Men gamble, I know. It's one of their many vices, but I fear it's become a... sickness for you. An addiction. I've loaned several—"

"Ah, so that's what this is about: your precious baubles. If a couple of gems are worth more to you than helping your dear father in his time of need, then perhaps you weren't raised as well as I thought. Maybe I shouldn't have accepted you into the Linton line, because we place great importance on blood. Something you don't seem to share."

The threat of cutting her out sliced at the scarred wounds of abandonment left by her biological mother, and Iris struggled to maintain her composure, fingernails digging into the leather chair arms as the hollow in her belly pitched in terror. She didn't want to lose Linton, even if he was an absent father. Even if he was a man who hadn't shown much attention to her in the short time of their acquaintance.

"I'll replace your little trinkets. Until then, please leave. I'm your father. You'd think I'd deserve more respect from a daughter. But I suppose I'm destined to be disappointed. Go now, Iris." He waved her off with disdain, terminating the discussion with the slam of a ledger as he pulled it from a corner of his desk.

Quaking with devastation, Iris forced her numb legs to stand and walk her out of the study, through the hall, and back to her carriage—a remarkable feat, considering her emotional turmoil.

What have I done?

Inside the closed carriage, she sat ramrod straight, gaze straight ahead to stare unseeing at the plush velvet pressed into a quilting pattern on the bench. Linton didn't want her. He thought *her* materialistic. Uncaring.

No one had ever described her in such a harsh fashion.

It was difficult to swallow... along with the bile gurgling in her throat.

Lord, she wished she were home in Shoreham again. Safe in the family cottage. Regretted praying so hard for a change this year. A self-deprecating snort erupted. *Change.* What a naïve and stupid wish.

I should've been more specific: change for the better.

Have you forgotten about your kind husband and his equally lovely mother?

It was true. She wouldn't have them if not for Linton, and the knowledge eased some of the melancholy dampening her spirits. Her father's words hurt, poked at old wounds, but she wouldn't trade this new life for her former one. Wasn't willing to never marry Clarke or meet Pru.

Life didn't play out like a romance novel. Some characters couldn't be redeemed or altered. And Iris feared that Linton might be one of them, no matter how hard she wished to have a loving relationship with every member of her family.

Somehow, she would need to learn how to make peace with her situation.

Linton may not want her, but Clarke and Pru and the rest of her large family did.

And they were enough.

Then why won't my heart stop aching for Linton?

CHAPTER TWENTY-ONE

Something is off with Iris.

S   Clarke felt it the moment he returned home and found her in the library window seat again. It seemed to be her escape to think after a negative experience. Inching into the room, he shut the door behind him and quietly joined her—kneeling at her feet like the first time he discovered her here.

"How was your day?" An innocuous question, but the perfect opportunity to confide in him.

"Fine. How was yours? Did your mother love hearing about the madness that is my family?" Her tone should've been teasing, playful. Instead, it bordered on melancholic, and Clarke's hackles rose another degree.

"She did. She also told me you visit her sometimes by yourself. I didn't know that."

"No?" Iris shrugged, tracing a seam on her dress. "It wasn't a secret. Your mother's the closest friend I have in London aside from you. She's very wise and easy to talk to."

Shame slicked his gut. Iris was used to being surrounded by a large, loving family, yet London provided none of those things. His mum and he were only two people, and he hadn't done a great job of being a confidante for her, either. The similarity to Linton in that aspect grated.

So much for your promise to introduce to her to more potential friends in your social circle.

He'd have to rectify that error as soon as possible.

"I'm sorry you've felt so isolated. I'll make more of an effort to come home earlier. To introduce you to more of my friends like I said I would. Because they're not all like the ones you met at the party. Lavinia. Johnson," he gritted out the last name, loathe to mention that bastard again.

"Thank you. I know you'll help however you can. And Porter's a good man, so the party wasn't a complete disaster..." Iris finally turned her head to meet his concerned gaze, and for the first time, he felt a brightening in her spirit. "On our wedding day, I actually overheard the two of you speaking about me. How you thought I was too frail to marry. I'm glad we've resolved that particular subject."

Yes, they had. With her bent before him as his cock fucked her sweet cunt into oblivion.

"You weren't supposed to hear that." Wry embarrassment brought a dark flush to his skin. "I don't believe you'll quite melt into pixie dust anymore, though this need to protect you will never go away. You'll always be my little sprite, no matter how capable I believe you to be. You can wrestle a hundred men to the ground, and I'd still think you the softest, most fragile part of my soul." It was the closest he'd come to voicing any sentiment close to love. A monumental shift of vulnerability for him.

"Protect me from every perceived villain as you see fit, as long as you don't count yourself among their ranks."

"Noted… Speaking of villains, why did you look so sad when I entered? Did someone say something to hurt you?" His money was on Linton.

Iris shook her head, brushing off the question. "It's of no concern. Especially when your challenge intrigues me."

"Challenge?" Clarke searched through their conversation, puzzled by the odd statement.

"You said even if I wrestled a hundred men to the ground, you'd still think me soft. Now, I'm curious to try wrestling just one man to the ground—you." Iris draped her legs over the edge of the seat before sliding to the floor, her thighs moving to bracket his. Shifting to a more secure position, Clarke readjusted to sit on the floor versus kneeling, causing his wife to lean more heavily on him.

Letting her avoid telling him what happened earlier probably wasn't a good idea, but how could he resist this transition from gloomy to naughty? If it made her feel better to fuck, who was he to refuse her? Especially after denying them for weeks before the trip to Hampshire.

"A little sprite like you doesn't stand much of a chance bringing me down, but you're welcome to try. I'm at your disposal." His arms widened, as if daring her to give it her best shot.

Which she promptly did, shoving his jacket off and unbuttoning his shirt so her hands could slide across his chest. "Excellent… Because all I want to do is explore my big…"

"Hulking."

"Strong…"

"Bullish."

"Husband."

"Well, I'll give you that one."

Sighing at his sarcasm, Iris bussed a kiss over his cheek. "I'm afraid no matter how much you try to deflect or act as if you're some terrible beast, you won't win. You can't fool me, Clarke."

That's what I'm afraid of.

"Do you remember that kiss we shared in the foyer? After my first visit to Linton's home, where I found it in disarray?"

"How could I forget? I came home to a disheveled washerwoman instead of my serene little wife. Why?"

Iris's hands pressed his arms to his sides, pinning them to the floor. "Because you held me against the wall just like this. Didn't let me touch you, and now it's my time to return the favor. You will keep your hands here until I say otherwise, understand?"

Since when did his sprite become so confident? So brazen?

Probably due to all the fucking in Hampshire. He'd created a seductive little sprite who belonged only to him.

"Understood," he agreed, his fingertips digging into the carpet beneath him.

Iris grinned in delight and massaged his shoulders. "Excellent. The lesson today is to teach you that my brand of strength can be just as effective as your brute power."

"You don't have to prove anything to me, sprite. I realize I've been too quick in my judgment of you—too narrow-minded by assessing you solely on your size." Iris held deep wells of strength and kindness, another type of asset in its own right.

"Nevertheless, I'm looking forward to conquering your challenge." The trail of her hair stimulated his nerve endings as she licked along his neck and chest, teasing a flat nipple for a response before mimicking the act on its twin. A sweet melody hummed in her throat, a tune only she knew, but one his heart began to follow as Iris continued her journey downward.

Dainty hands began to unfasten his trousers. *Surely, she isn't...* But it appeared she was as Clarke felt the heated breath of his wife wash over his thick erection. "Iris, do you know what you're doing?"

"In theory... But don't worry, I'm open to your instruction." A saucy wink stunned him into submission, his head tipping backwards to the floor at the sultriness of her tone. *The little minx would kill him with that pretty mouth of hers.*

And all he really had to say about it was a prayer of thanks sent swiftly up to God.

In retrospect, it was surprising they hadn't partaken in this particular pleasure at the Trent home, but Clarke could only blame himself for being too greedy. He wanted to lick the honey between her thighs, then bury himself there—didn't leave much room for her to explore.

The swipe of a hot tongue lapped at the mushroom head of his cock, swallowing the drops of seed gleaming at its tip. Two hands enveloped him in a secure grip—much firmer than the first time Iris held him in the carriage after their run-in with Johnson. Indeed, she knew what he preferred in spades.

Staring up at the vaulted ceiling, Clarke's hands fisted at his sides, determined to give her this, to not interfere. But it was damned difficult when his wife began suckling in earnest, her pouty mouth drawing on him enthusiastically.

And the sounds.

A fucking obscene song of sex and carnality that brought him to the precipice of release embarrassingly fast. His abdomen tightened. He forced air through his nose, counting the harsh breaths. Anything to make this last longer for the both of them.

But then Iris reached beneath his cock to roll his stones together, exploring the different texture, and his control snapped. Bucking up into her mouth, Clarke growled—his throat straining under the impact of his orgasm, and long jets of his seed surged forward. To Iris's credit, she tried swallowing it all, but a goodly amount slipped past her lips and down her chin, creating a filthy picture of overindulgence and debauchery.

When she was finally satisfied with her handiwork, she eased up his prone body and nuzzled into his neck. "See? I've got a power all my own."

"Bloody hell... you don't have to tell me twice." Because his wife was magic—pure and simple. A sprite who deigned to keep him company, and hell would come to whoever dared harm her.

CHAPTER TWENTY-TWO

Three days passed in a contented haze as Iris and Clarke enjoyed outings to the park together or quiet evenings in where she'd read passages from her current book aloud. It almost resembled her former fantasies of what marriage would be like, except she never accounted for the enormous amount of animal spirits her husband possessed—or that she held, too, for that matter. Because each interlude ended with a fiery kiss or a secretive touch in a wholly inappropriate location if they were out in public.

It was sheer bliss.

Until Linton appeared one afternoon, hat in hand, to dampen the idyllic feeling she'd been drifting in.

No note. No warning. And Iris prayed this was a sign of his impending apology. Of his devotion to turning over a new leaf.

"Good afternoon, Father," she said, sweeping into the room as if she were a queen instead of the lowly servant girl she felt like in his presence.

"Hullo, dear." Linton waited for her to sit before settling himself, a sheepish expression transforming his florid features. "I've come to beg your forgiveness. There's no defense for how I treated you the other day, other than I've had a lot on my mind these past two weeks. You were only offering assistance where none was needed, and instead of explaining the situation calmly, I flew off the handle."

Relief poured through her veins like the first refreshing rainfall after a drought. "All is forgiven. I didn't approach the subject very well either. I didn't mean to seem accusatory."

"I understand. Water under the bridge, eh?" He winked, and she noticed a strange light enter his eyes. "On a separate note, you mentioned a birthday celebration? A dinner? I hope it's not too late to take you up on that. It'd be lovely to spend more time with you."

Immensely pleased with the admission, Iris eagerly nodded, ignoring the bell of warning at the back of her mind. *This is too fast. Too easy. There's more to discuss.* Which can occur in due time.

Perhaps she was rushing things. Iris should be grateful for a reconciliation. Keep their relationship on steady ground where it can grow, then slowly try to rehabilitate his compulsion to gamble.

"I'd love to host a birthday dinner for you. I'll even invite my sisters and their families, so everyone can reacquaint themselves."

"Capital idea, my dear! Now..." Linton reached in his jacket pocket and pulled out a scrap of paper with a scribbled name on it. He gave it to Iris, his sweaty palm blurring the address, though it remained legible. "This is a favorite flower shop of mine. They've always stocked the Linton home, and I feel it's only right to continue using their services. Especially for such a momentous occasion."

"Of course." Iris carefully folded the sheet. "I'll visit tomorrow afternoon to ensure they're able to provide everything that will be needed."

"That's my girl." Linton rose and proffered his arms for an embrace, which Iris hastily accepted. "Well, it's time for me to take my leave, let you prepare for tomorrow and the party. And thank you again, my dear. You're a true Linton, after all."

Beaming, Iris hugged the high praise close to her chest.

Acceptance.

Finally.

THE NEXT MORNING, IRIS awakened with an extra bounce in her step. She'd shared the news of a birthday dinner with Clarke the night before, and he'd immediately supported her efforts, despite the animosity between him and Linton. He was careful to hide his true feelings for her father most days, but she wasn't oblivious to his dislike of the man. An enmity due to Linton's treatment of her so far, which she couldn't exactly fault her husband for.

Wading through Bond Street was a breeze as the sidewalks remained empty of most of London's elite. *Too busy sleeping off the festivities of last evening*, Iris thought. *Or possibly afraid of being caught in a rainstorm.* Her gaze studied the grey clouds covering the city, and she hastened her steps as did the maid who accompanied her.

Clarke's latest addition to her security.

Perhaps I should've waited until this afternoon for a visit to avoid the rain.

But she'd been too excited to start on Linton's party. Besides, what difference did a few hours make?

Potentially becoming a soggy mess, for starters.

She'd told Jimmy to circle the neighborhood rather than waiting for them outside the flower shop—no need for such fuss when it wouldn't take long to place an order with the shopkeeper. "Come along, Nancy. I might have misjudged how much time we'd have before the heavens open with a deluge to soak us through to the bone."

"Yes, ma'am." The young woman lifted her skirts and hurried alongside Iris, both of them focused on the stone walk rather than their destination ahead. Until two men stinking of tobacco stepped in front of them, blocking their way.

"Oh, excuse us." Iris tried to sidestep the strangers.

"Don't think so, lady," one snarled as his hands constricted around her arm. The other stranger tossed Nancy to the ground, where she landed in a heap of skirts with a yelp.

"You're comin' with us." Suddenly an unmarked carriage appeared, and a third man tossed her captor a rope. Struggling under his tight hold, Iris fought to escape, a scream cut off by a wet cloth stuffed in her mouth. "Uh uh. Keep your mouth shut and no harm will come to you."

Not bloody likely.

A masculine shout hollered down the road, and Iris caught sight of Jimmy racing the horses down the street.

"Hurry up! We haven't got all day!" Grubby hands dragged her into the cab, kneeling on her back as her face scraped along the floor. Wooziness permeated her limbs, her mind becoming fuzzy as an awful flavor coated her tongue.

What did they use to drug me?

Iris maintained enough consciousness to pray for Jimmy's arrival until a shot rang out, and the wheels beneath her began pounding over cobblestones. The jostling ride did nothing to help her sluggishness except add nausea to the growing list of aches pervading her body.

Rest. Perhaps this is a dream. Rest.

So, Iris closed her eyes and mumbled a discordant prayer before blacking out into nothingness.

Please let this be a dream.

CHAPTER TWENTY-THREE

Clarke returned home to a panicked household. Two maids cried in a corner while Jimmy spoke with a tall man who appeared to be a constable with his tell-tale uniform.

"What the devil's going on here?" he shouted above the din. His day had already been full of headaches from learning of a failed venture in Guatemala to his barrister informing him of his retirement. All he wanted now was some peace and quiet with his wife. Was that too much to ask?

"Oh, sir! It's terrible! Just terrible!" The younger of the two maids stepped forward, a handkerchief held to her red nose as harsh sobs wracked her body. "Right in front of me. And gone. Oh, it's terrible!"

He tried to decipher the woman's words through her tears but failed and turned in exasperation to the policeman and Jimmy. "Care to explain what's so terrible?"

"It appears your wife was taken this morning following a visit to the flower shop. Your man here was just giving me his statement of events."

Iris.

Taken?

"By whom? Who the hell kidnapped my wife?" Fury burned a path down his spine, his muscles blazing with the need to punish whoever dared to touch Iris. To take her from him.

"They left this note on the sidewalk after shooting at poor Jimmy. Fortunately, he only sustained minor injuries, but the shot spooked the horses enough that he couldn't pursue her captors. Isn't that right?" The investigator motioned to the coachman, who nodded while handing Clarke a crumpled sheet of paper. Snatching it out of the man's hand, he finally noticed the black eye blooming on Jimmy's face, as well.

Bring 10,000 pounds to the corner of Kenniston and Hobbes by midnight or else Mrs. Calloway will suffer.

He crushed the threat. *If they harmed Iris...* No, he couldn't allow himself to dwell on the possibility, or else he'd be no help at all to her. Why her? Why ten thousand pounds?

It was an exorbitant amount, double what he'd paid her father to marry her.

Something niggled at his memory. "Why was my wife at the flower shop so early? She'd planned on visiting later this afternoon."

And why wasn't I notified until now?

Perhaps Jimmy was only now able to make it home with the carriage and horses.

Perhaps they couldn't find him in his office.

Does it really matter? You know now.

"She was excited to start working on the marquess's party and left earlier. His lordship suggested the shop, and Mrs. Calloway didn't want to take the chance they wouldn't be able to fulfill the order," the second maid piped up from the corner.

"My father-in-law mentioned the shop?" A sick feeling grew in his gut at the girl's confirmation. Linton didn't bother with menial tasks such as flower shopping. How would he know which shop to recommend?

Unless he had a specific purpose for sending Iris there in the first place.

"I believe I have a lord to question, then. Sir," he gestured to the constable. "You should come with me."

"At your service. The name's Charles Hinch. Perhaps you can explain how his lordship will help?"

"He's the man who set up my wife, and if his creditors don't kill him, I will."

Clarke ran to collect his horse, who hadn't even been properly stabled yet in the short time span he'd arrived home, and he and Mr. Hinch rode for Linton Place.

Because that son of a bitch sold her again.

Clarke told Hinch through intermittent spurts about Linton's gambling problem and history of selling his newfound daughter to the highest bidder as they trotted towards Linton's. "I've no doubt he bargained with these men to kidnap Iris and ensure my ransom as part of his debt repayment."

"Sounds like a bastard," Hinch muttered before conversation became impossible, the skies releasing a torrential downpour of pelting rain.

Fuck.

Weaving around closed carriages and strollers caught unawares by the weather, they entered a middling part of town—the only area Linton could afford at this point, despite Clarke's infusion of cash.

Tying his horse to a balustrade, he took the stone steps leading to the entry two at a time and tried the brass doorknob, forgoing niceties such as knocking. The door swung open with a bang, and Clarke yelled for Linton the moment he stepped through the entry, leaving puddles of water in his wake.

"Linton, you fucking bastard. Get down here and tell me what you've done with my wife!"

The grey-haired man slipped out of a side door down the hall, guilt written on his wrinkled features. "Mr. Calloway. Clarke." He lifted his hands in placation at Clarke's hasty advance. "Hold on a moment. Let me explain. They won't hurt her. She'll be fine once they get their money. I was desperate! They threatened—"

"I don't give a damn what they threatened to do to you. You should've been more afraid of me." Clarke's palm wrapped around Linton's throat, shoving him into the wall which sent a painted landscape clattering to the floor. "Who has Iris? My men at the Beckman Den haven't reported anything amiss, so who else do you owe?"

Linton gasped for air, sputtering out a few words. "It's Beckman. They know about the surveillance, which is why we had to set up a rendezvous point at a separate location."

"How many men will be there? What should I expect? And don't lie to me." Clarke tightened his grip, and Linton turned an unbecoming shade of red, sweat dotting his forehead.

"Two. There should only be two men. They promised not to hurt her. I asked them not to—"

"Fool! Do you think they'll honor the requests of an indebted man?" Clarke growled. "Do you think they possess any honor at all when they're willing to kidnap a woman—*my* woman? You disgust me." Releasing the old man with a scoff, Linton collapsed to the floor as Clarke whipped around to find a wall of servants watching, along with Hinch in the background.

"Most definitely a bastard," Hinch said when their gazes met over the startled heads of Linton's staff, and Clarke almost grinned at the matter-of-fact tone.

"Agreed. Now, let's save my wife."

CHAPTER TWENTY-FOUR

Slick stone chilled her cheek. Blinking past the pain emanating from her head, Iris opened her eyes to see the gleam of cobblestones beneath her palm. The gentle pitter-patter of rain landed in puddles beside her while sliding over her forehead and into her eyes.

Where am I?

She searched for clues, trying to recall her last memory. Her father's birthday dinner. The flower shop. Two men who'd shoved a damp cloth in her mouth, turning everything black.

And now she was here. Outside in the rain. Lying prone on the ground.

"I don't understand why we have to wait in the bloody rain. I'm freezing my ballocks off out here!" The whiny male voice came from her left. Followed by the snap of his companion.

"How many times do I have to explain we can't go to the den? That hulking cove of hers has men watching it, or would you rather get caught and be strung up by your toes?"

Hulking cove.

That would be her husband.

Clarke knew these men? He'd hired people to keep an eye on them? Why?

A question for another time, she decided. Of imminent importance was gaining her freedom. In her sprawled position,

Iris realized her captors hadn't bothered to keep her restrained. Clearly, she offered no threat of escape in their mind.

Mildly irritated by the lack of concern—everyone underestimated her due to her looks and diminutive size—she nevertheless promised to make them regret the oversight. *If I can figure out an escape...*

They appeared to be sequestered in an alley located in the textile district if the stacks of smoke billowing upward and the smell of turpentine meant anything. Was it after work hours? During a shift?

She wished she knew how long she'd lain unconscious. With the dreary overcast sky, it was impossible to determine the time of day, and she didn't know if a mere shout for help would bring anyone to the rescue if there was no one about to hear her call.

"Oi, look who's awake, Tim." A pair of old boots came into view, their soles slapping the ground separately from the leather they should've been attached to. The complaining man of earlier squatted before her and grinned, his brown teeth sending a shudder down her spine, and with her movements sighted, Iris slowly pushed to her knees.

"Enjoy your nap, lovey? You might be in for a longer one if your man doesn't give us what we want."

"And what is it that you want, sir?" Money, most likely, since she didn't have anything else of value to offer anyone, but their confirmation may give her insight as to why they chose her as the woman to hold for ransom.

"Don't get your knickers in a twist. We just want what's owed to us by your dear papa." The lead man, Tim, snickered, and her stomach sank.

Oh, Father, what have you done?

She'd helped him in the past. They'd moved on from their spat. Yet somehow, he hadn't mentioned needing more money during his last visit. *He gave you the shop address instead.* The act held a suspicious light now as she remembered the fidgety energy that shrouded him.

No. Surely, he wouldn't be a part of this.

"If you're counting on him arriving with cash in hand, I'm afraid you'll be waiting for a while. My father is penniless and hardly cares for me enough to beg for a ransom from who's left of his friends. We've only known each other a few short months, after all."

"Oh, we know all about your arrangement. That's why we're waiting on your husband to pay up. He's the one with real blunt to spend, and by the looks of those marks on your neck, he'll only be too happy to oblige us." A disgusting leer traced the love bites Clarke had left the night before. Her masking powder must have washed off in the rain.

Bringing a hand to her neck in an attempt to hide them from this stranger, Iris glared at the men, shaking away the continuing fall of droplets threatening to blind her. "I wouldn't count on his benevolence if I were you. Clarke can be quite feral when needed. And dealing with a couple of rotten kidnappers would definitely call for ferocity."

"I wouldn't be insulting us, bitch. We're liable to dump you in the river for your lip."

"And lose out on your ransom? I don't think so." Iris braced a hand on the slippery brick wall to her side and stood with wobbly legs—whatever they'd dosed her with hadn't fully worn off yet, it seemed. Fatigue and dizziness warred with the icy numbness saturating her body as uncontrollable shivering shook her limbs. Lots of good her layered skirts were doing—a heavy anchor of ice—she felt encased in a frosty tomb. *And at the tail end of spring, too.*

Teeth chattering, Iris kept talking as her gaze swept the alley, scouting for an exit. "How much does my father owe you? Tell me what I'm worth to him and my husband." No such luck to her right; it led to a dead-end with another building topped with smokestacks. A street appeared to her left around fifteen meters away, but she'd have to distract her captors while managing a run in her condition—not to mention the unceasing deluge from above.

You can do this. You're no shrinking violet.

The strength emboldening her limbs and words came from deep within Iris. From a place she'd never tapped into before but found quite useful. Sometimes a firmer hand was needed, especially when dealing with criminals. Her usually quiet demeanor would not work in her favor here.

"Ten thousand pounds."

Twice as much as Clarke had paid him for her hand in marriage, an astounding amount. Her father had a gambling problem. She knew he did, had warned him of it. And despite his lack of acknowledgment of the problem, it hurt that he couldn't curb himself, even to pacify Iris. Couldn't stop himself from falling into a deadly game where the only way out would be through selling his daughter. *Again.*

"What's wrong with me?" she whispered mournfully. Her mother abandoned her days after she was born, and her newfound father didn't care about her, regardless of all she'd done to earn his affection. Iris had married a stranger, for goodness's sake! But it hadn't been enough.

Never enough.

The men started arguing when the one complained again about the weather. Thankful for the diversion, a calm settled over her—or perhaps hypothermia was setting in—and she concentrated on the road ahead. Fifteen meters. Hardly a distance for a country girl such as herself.

Iris spared one last glance at her jailers before jetting forward, sticking close to the wall for support. Shouts of displeasure erupted behind her, but she didn't allow herself to look back. *Keep going. One foot in front of the other.* Except the toe of her boot caught on an uneven stone, sending her sprawling to the ground with a harsh thud.

Agony radiated up her hands and knees—the rough impact immobilizing her until a hard kick landed on her hip, and Iris tumbled to her back, breathless.

"Thought you could get away? A little pigeon like you?" Tim sneered and nudged her with his foot. Bruising would surely mottle her side, along with red scrapes furrowing her palms and forearms.

Clarke won't like this.

And she almost smiled. A daft tilting of her lips belying all that had befallen her.

Because the situation reeked of irony.

Clarke had been so careful of her—afraid to injure her with the slightest touch. Yet here she lay, beaten red and blue. Despite his best efforts, danger marred her skin, after all.

But I'm not broken.

Like she'd told Clarke she wouldn't be by his touch.

Like she believed she wouldn't be when push came to shove.

Iris had always trusted her strength, even if it manifested in a less demonstrative way than her more outgoing sisters. Now, she had a body of proof.

Literally.

CHAPTER TWENTY-FIVE

The street lay deserted when Clarke and Hinch arrived. With work shifts complete and the scream of stormy weather, no one dared to linger outside, hobnobbing about.

Which suits me just fine.

They dismounted their horses at the corner adjacent to the appointed rendezvous spot, but the area remained empty except for them. Where was Iris? Shaking the rain out of his eyes, Clarke checked his pocket watch, struggling to decipher the time underneath the haze of water, but the hands said five minutes until the proposed meeting time.

Surely, he hadn't beaten the kidnappers to the location.

"I'm going to try to circle around the back of the building." Hinch pointed to the tall structure butting up to the corner. "See if I can't surprise anyone who's lurking."

Nodding, Clarke said, "Good luck," before crossing the street and heading towards the lamppost at the corner. But as he crossed the end of an alley, muffled words filtered through the clamor of rain. Glancing down the dark corridor, he considered ignoring the supposed sound, ready to chalk it up to his imagination, when a distinctly feminine whimper followed.

Iris.

His eyes narrowed as he searched in vain for her. Nightfall and rain made vision beyond a few meters near impossible, especially with the streetlight so far away. He'd be at a disadvantage entering without an idea of who waited for him where. However, fear wasn't his chief emotion. Vengeance was.

Linton said two men would be waiting for him.

Well, they were in for a devil of a night because a blistering fire rose so quickly within him, he wouldn't have been surprised to witness steam coming off his skin.

Creeping forward, Clarke kept his steps light and a hand to the brick wall beside him. Everyone would be affected by the worsened conditions, but at least he'd heard them before declaring himself. He held the upper hand as long as the element of surprise stuck by his side.

As Clarke snuck deeper into the alley, the voices became clearer until he could just make out two forms arguing ahead. One man his height but leaner, the other short and stout.

Too easy.

But where was his wife?

A constant click-clacking sound didn't match the pattern of rain on the tin roofs above, and as he searched for the source, another whimper reached him. There. A small form lay huddled on the ground, hugging the wall—from his vantage point, Clarke could make out the incessant shivers wracking the body. He realized the persistent click-clacking was Iris's teeth chattering from the cold.

These bastards kidnapped my wife and left her to freeze to death.

They couldn't even be bothered to find a dry spot to wait for him.

Imbeciles.

Dead imbeciles.

Crouching to the ground, Clarke swept his hands over the cobblestone, hunting for a weapon when he brushed against a stray brick. *It'll have to do.* He hefted the brick into his palm and homed in on his target—the tall man who seemed to be the leader based on the irate tone he used with his cohort.

"Stop complaining before I cut your tongue out. If you're so lily-livered that a good dose of rain does you in, run on back to the den. Billy will have a field day learning one of his men ain't worth his weight."

Billy Beckman. Owner of a gambling hell and home to his nefarious gang. A more dissolute establishment would be hard to find. No wonder Linton caved to their demands so easily.

He'll pay for his part in this soon enough.

Focus.

Like a leopard in the rainforest, Clarke's muscles tensed under his shirt and jacket, the soaked materials molding to his body. Everything faded except for his prey.

The rain. The chill in his bones.

Every cell focused on protecting Iris.

His wife.

His love.

The man started walking towards him, clearly heading to the rendezvous, and Clarke felt a vibration of energy run beneath his skin like an unearthly spirit possessed him. A demon from hell come to reassert its claim on his fallen angel.

Leaping from his position, Clarke rammed his target into the wall and brought the brick down on his temple with a roar of rage.

The bastard dropped like a stone.

"Now... Now, mister... I don't want any part of this. Take the girl. You can have her. Just let me—"

The blubbering idiot must have realized Clarke wasn't in a negotiating mood. Because he stopped pleading and started praying, stumbling back until he hit the wall marking the alley's end. Trapped. Like a vile little rat.

"Your friend was right. You are lily-livered. Too bad you got into the wrong kind of business. And it's doubly a shame that you chose to take my wife from me. To harm what's mine," Clarke growled, low and deadly.

Hand raised high above his head, he swung the brick down to dispense with this last obstacle between him and Iris. Except a shout of warning erupted behind him.

"Mr. Calloway, stop!" Hinch had arrived. He must have discovered the lack of another entry and circled back around the building. "Don't kill him! You don't need two men's blood on your hands. Let me arrest him for kidnapping and attempted blackmail. You'll still get your justice."

Justice would be this cowering man's blood joining the piss surely seeping down his leg, the stench overpowering in the constricted space.

"He's... right... Clarke." His concentration shattered at Iris's trembling voice. The brick fell from numb hands as he whirled to the right and dropped to his knees, hauling her into his arms.

"Oh, my darling. I'm so sorry. Tell me where it hurts." He tore his jacket off to wrap it around her body, but the drenched cloth wasn't much help at retaining warmth. Lifting her in his arms, he bypassed Hinch, who held the remaining kidnapper under custody, and retrieved his horse, securing Iris to him before heading home.

"My head is pounding from whatever they subdued me with," Iris whispered, her cold nose burrowing into his neck. "Are Nancy and Jimmy alright? I heard a gunshot before losing consciousness."

"They're fine. A little banged up but fine." Cuddling her close, conversation paused while the rain continued to douse them. Upon returning home, the entire staff greeted them before bombarding Iris and him with hot towels, dry clothes, and lemongrass tea.

A doctor arrived and confined Iris to bedrest for a few days, especially after examining the dark bruising around her ribs and hip. Clarke regretted not killing her second captor once those were revealed. The purple wounds carved into his heart never to be forgotten.

When everyone was as dry and as healthy as they could be for the evening, Clarke joined Iris in her bed, smoothing a tender hand over her blonde hair. "Rest, little sprite. I'll be here to watch over you." And with an adorable yawn, Iris listened, nestling into his embrace as he kept vigil over his precious wife.

CHAPTER TWENTY-SIX

"Your father arranged the kidnapping," Clarke stated bluntly the following morning, the concern in his eyes softening the blow. Though hearing confirmation of what Iris feared wasn't as debilitating as she expected.

She'd grown in the past few months. While her issues with abandonment had risen to the forefront, so had knowledge of her inner strength and determination. Of her worth.

She'd fought for her father's affection.

Fought to prove to him that she was a daughter worth knowing.

Yet he'd still betrayed her.

"I figured as much," Iris admitted, resting her head on Clarke's strong shoulder, breathing in his comforting scent. "The marquess has a problem. A disease. And I'm afraid I'm not the cure as much as I'd hoped to be."

It was the first time she'd referred to her father by his title, distancing herself from the familial connection the lord claimed only to abuse.

"It was never your responsibility—never in your capabilities—to do such a thing, love. He was a lost cause long before he crashed into your life." Clarke smoothed a hand over her head before kissing her temple. The warmth of his body and the glowing fire finally chased the last of her chill away, and she snuggled deeper into the shelter of her husband's arms. Her body continued to ache from the events of yesterday, but her heart felt lighter.

"I understand that now."

Linton was only a man. One who had fathered her over twenty years ago, but she didn't need anything more from him. Not anymore.

He'd given her Clarke—a fortuitous arrangement that filled her heart with love and devotion.

And she knew he felt the same.

Iris didn't need to fear being abandoned or left behind because her husband would never leave her. He'd proven he'd always come for her, no matter the circumstances.

Between him and her sisters, her life was whole.

And Linton's stronghold on her emotions evaporated like a morning fog in the spring.

"How do you feel? Still cold? Hungry?" Clarke offered another strawberry from the breakfast tray, but she declined.

"No, I'm feeling better than I have in a long time. Linton's arrival in my life confused me and made me forget that I already had a wonderful Papa. A loving one who accepted me into his home as a true daughter from day one." Iris reminisced about her childhood in Shoreham. Idyllic and full of caring. And never once a snide comment about her origins.

She'd forgotten those happier times. Allowed her fears and doubts to take root. "And now I have you." Iris met Clarke's dark gaze with fondness, sliding a wayward lock off his forehead. "A man I love," she admitted aloud, and his reaction was immediate.

Twisting her around in his lap until she faced him, his grip on her waist tightened though he was careful to avoid the spot where Tim kicked her, and a rumble of pleasure emanated from his chest. "What did you just say?"

"I love you, Clarke Calloway. Possessive. Protective. You are my strong, ferocious husband, and I will never want another. I'm yours." She had been from the start. Ever since she'd eavesdropped on his conversation and heard the reverence in his voice. Even when he'd kept a wall between them out of fear of harming her.

She'd been his.

Nostrils flaring, Clarke stared unblinking at her soft but resolute expression. "You love me. You're mine," he repeated, as if the words weren't quite registering.

"Yes, I am, and honestly, the being *yours* part shouldn't be so shocking. You've certainly demanded I say it enough times when we make love."

"But I've never heard you say it in conjunction with being in love with me." He nuzzled her cheek with his nose, drawing his mouth up to her ear until he could whisper, "I never imagined a sweet little sprite like you could love someone like me. Never dared to dream of such a thing, but that didn't stop me from falling for you. I've been under your spell from the moment you walked down the aisle towards me—gowned in cream silk and shining brighter than any star in the sky."

A shuddering breath ran through him. "I belong to you as surely as you belong to me, Iris Calloway. My love for you is unending and true. You will never be alone again. Unless there's an act of God, you never need to fear an existence without me by your side." Then he chuckled. "And even then, I'll probably return to watch over you since I can't be too long from my darling sprite."

"I don't doubt it." She adjusted her head so their lips could meet in a promise of forever. Confident and firm, Clarke buried a hand in her hair and took charge. Unfortunately, an insistent knocking at the bedroom door interrupted them before long, and Iris pulled away with a giggle.

"We're needed... Clarke..."

He kept pressing kiss after kiss to her lips and cheeks and anywhere else he could reach, instead. "Ignore them. What I need is you in our bed, naked and writhing beneath me as I eat your sweet cunt. Everyone else can wait."

The filthy vow sent her temperature soaring while an aroused flush dove below to slicken her thighs. She was about to heartily agree with his suggestion when another knock sounded on the door.

"I'm sorry to disturb the two of you, especially after your ordeal, Mrs. Calloway, but Lord Linton is downstairs demanding to see you," Mrs. Franklin said through the wood paneling and shock paralyzed Iris. How dare he come to their home and make demands after his role in her kidnapping!

Clarke must have formed the same conclusion because his body stiffened, and she found herself gently removed from his lap. "That fucking bastard is in our home?" Rampaging like a careening wagon rolling unchecked down a hill, he tromped out of the room in a fury, with Iris following close at his heels.

They both stopped at the double-door entry to their parlor, side by side—one breathing harshly while the other remained remarkably calm. Linton, for his part, heard them barreling down the stairs and stood to greet them, an expression of despair on his worn features. This wasn't the same enigmatic man who'd approached her months ago about her heritage or her impending nuptials. Not a man of noble birth with all the dignity it bestowed upon him.

No, this was a broken old man whose desperation clung to his aura like dung to a boot.

"What motive could you possibly have for coming here?" Clarke barked, taking a step forward. "Isn't it enough that Iris almost died from exposure due to you? Now, you've returned... For what purpose?"

"I'm truly sorry for the injury you've been dealt, my dear." Linton adjusted his weight from one foot to the other, a cane clenched in his right hand. "I never meant for any harm to befall you, though I realize now my folly in believing that would be the case." He cleared his throat with a cough. "Unfortunately, the original reason for your capture remains at large, and while I hate to burden you again, I must beg for assistance."

"You still need to repay Beckman," Clarke surmised.

With a tilt of his chin, Linton confirmed the assessment. "I humbly lay myself at your feet—prevailing upon your Christian duty, if not familial love."

"You're damn right there's no familial love here. And Christian duty seems to be lacking, too. You'll not get a shilling from us. Iris deserves more than what you've deemed to give her. Scraps of affection dangled before her for your manipulation. Well, no longer. You're done hurting my wife. Thank your lucky stars she's not pressing charges for your role in her capture and leave. You're not welcome here."

Love for her husband bloomed in her chest, deepening the adoration she felt for him, as his protective instincts came to full mast. Iris had never felt so well cared for in her life, and she had to swallow past the lump in her throat and blink away tears. Imbued with Clarke's love and her epiphany of worth, she glided forward, placing a gentle hand on her husband's arm.

"Thank you, my love. But I can handle him now." She would show Linton that he hadn't beaten her, that she wasn't an unworthy, unwanted child anymore. "We will pay your debt and for a trip to the Continent where you will be left to your own devices away from the lure of London." Clarke started to object, but she shook her head. They would do this one last time because she couldn't live with herself if something happened to Linton while it was in her power to stop it. It wasn't capitulation; it was grace. Kindness.

Characteristics Iris tried every day to exude. Linton wouldn't change that.

"But it will be the final saving of your hide. If you choose to continue to gamble your life away, that is your choice, and you must live with the consequences. But I'm hoping a leave of London and your former creditors will do you good. As for our blood connection, I don't see our relationship deepening until substantial changes have been made in your life and character. Perhaps even then I won't be able to allow you back into my life, but I won't rule out a reconciliation at this time." Exhaling the vestiges of their tattered bond, Iris smiled serenely, no longer bound by guilt or shame or fear.

She turned her back on the man who'd claimed to be her father—a man who'd sought to use her instead of loving her—and faced Clarke, the true hero in her eyes. Holding a hand out, she asked, "Shall we return to our previous engagement, love? I think we're finished here."

Clarke grinned, taking her hand in a firm grasp, and they left the parlor—left the Marquess of Linton sputtering, alone and forgotten.

CHAPTER TWENTY-SEVEN

If my cock's not buried in this woman within the next five minutes, I won't be responsible for my actions.

Iris's showdown with her father had been magnificent. If they hadn't already been wed, Clarke would've married her on the spot just from witnessing her righteous strength and beauty in action.

"I hope it wasn't too presumptuous announcing we'd pay Linton's debt and for a trip to the Continent. I know it's your money, and he's *my* problem—"

"Get on the bed and spread your knees, sprite. We're done talking about Linton. You're free to do as you wish, because everything I own is yours." If it made her feel better—providing her father with this final boon—then so be it. Her happiness was what mattered to him most. "Now, do as I say, and love? Spread them wide. I want to see every glistening pink inch of your pussy prepared for my tongue."

Edging backward, she lay on the bed, a cloud of uncertainty warring with desire. "You're sure? You said he wouldn't get a shilling more, then I turned around and contradicted you."

"Sweetheart, all I care about is devouring your wet cunt while my name falls from your lips as you beg for more. Is that clear?"

An impish smile washed away her doubt. "Crystal." And she lifted her gown to expose pale thighs before bending her knees and letting them fall open for his viewing pleasure.

Bloody hell, he adored his wife.

Petite and ethereal. Soft and tender, inside and out. He could stare at her for an eternity and never have enough. Still discover new freckles or lines or curves to explore.

"You are too good for this world, love. It's a fucking miracle that I found you."

"And paid for me." A lascivious wiggle accompanied the harsh fact, though her tone added a salacious layer to the truth. Like he owned her. Like she was bought for his pleasure alone.

"Careful, little sprite..." he warned her, though he knew now she wasn't as frail as he'd once thought. His woman exuded feminine strength and could handle him at his worst. Loved him at his most wicked.

"Or else... What?" Her hips arched forward, trying to tempt him over the edge of control. "You'll ravish me? Devour me in one bite?"

Stalking to the end of the bed, Clarke grabbed her ankles and yanked her closer to him, tangling the nightgown underneath her. This boldness never failed to surprise him. She'd grown confident in her seductive skills each time they were together—venturing to voice her desires more explicitly with every bout of lovemaking. It seemed Iris was no longer afraid of saying what she wanted, however brazen it may be.

And he adored it.

"Perhaps..." he drawled. His lips skimmed the delicate bones of her ankle, delighting in the gasp of surprise emitted from above. "I think that's what you need from me, wife. A reminder of who you belong to. A hard fucking to prove you're mine." He nipped her thigh before sucking the abused flesh between his lips to leave another mark of ownership.

Rising swiftly, Clarke eyed his handiwork. Then his gaze traveled higher to stop at its fading twin on her neck. *That won't do.*

Iris needed a visible brand of his possession at all times. He didn't care how barbaric it made him.

"Don't I say it enough times when we're in bed? I'm yours, Clarke. No other man will do."

"No other man will ever get a chance to."

Iris's legs fell further apart as she ran her hands over her breasts, teasing the nipples. "Best prove yourself then."

And so he did.

Until his prediction came true and his wife screamed for more from her husband, who was only too happy to oblige.

EPILOGUE ONE

THREE MONTHS LATER

"We have a secret to share with you, Mum." Clarke squeezed Iris's hand in his as they both cast a conspiratorial grin his mother's way. "Your wish will finally become reality because we're expecting a child."

A squeal of glee erupted so loudly that Maude came running from the hall to ensure everything was alright. "We're fine, Maude. Just expecting a baby! I knew it wouldn't take long for you to gift your old mother with a grandchild." Pru nodded meaningfully. "You never could stop yourself from fulfilling my every whim that was within your power."

"A flaw to be sure," he teased, content with the knowledge that he couldn't deny any of his women their heart's desire. And if this baby would be no different once born. *A spoiled little prince or princess.* But in the best of ways.

"Have you told your family yet, dear?" his mother asked Iris, who shook her head in the negative.

"No, not yet. We want to do it in person, which is another reason why we wanted to visit today. We'd like you to come to Hampshire with us." Iris had convinced him it would be safe, and he'd thought to himself how easily he could obtain a comfortable train car for his mum and Maude. The four of them could safely travel to the country together, his mother enjoying her first trip out of London in years.

"You do?" She glanced questioningly at him, and he nodded in approval. The brightest smile he'd ever seen lit her wrinkled cheeks as her fingers snapped in excitement. "Maude, we have much to do. We're going on a holiday." The two women discussed arrangements while Clarke turned to Iris, his hand moving to cover her slightly round belly.

"One down, only a dozen more people to go," he teased, referring to their large network of family. Travers and Hazel had visited them the month prior from Manchester, and he'd learned more about the factory Travers planned on building with a man named Riverton. It felt good discussing business affairs with the younger man, forming a friendship beyond their in-law obligations.

"It'll be a circus in Shoreham, no doubt..." Iris bit her lip as her features darkened in thought. "Do you think I should write Linton to notify him of the news? The baby *will* be his first grandchild." They hadn't spoken to the marquess since his wife had banished the man to Europe—a task that had improved her spirits immensely after she'd confided how often Linton had requested money from her. Clarke's gut still tightened in anger, realizing how much of a burden Iris had carried by herself because she hadn't felt she could enlist his help.

Not since he'd kept a distance between them due to his misconception about her strength.

Stupid bastard.

But at least he'd seen the error of his ways. The same couldn't be said for the marquess.

Clarke had maintained tabs on Linton, and the old fool was running amok around the Continent, racking up debts. It was only a matter of time before they caught up to him. And Clarke would be here to console Iris, even if she had chosen to relinquish their relationship.

"It's up to you, my love. I'll support whatever you decide." He always would.

Because Clarke loved Iris beyond what he even thought possible, his heart beating for his little sprite alone.

A woman he may have bought for selfish reasons, but who'd completely claimed his soul, instead.

"I'll think about it some more before deciding... I love you and our little one. I only want to do what's best for our family," she whispered.

"I trust your judgment, sprite. You always do the right thing. That's what makes us such a good pair. You balance out my scoundrel tendencies."

Iris scoffed before glancing towards his mother and Maude, who were still occupied by their animated conversation. "Don't be ridiculous. You were never a scoundrel with me, no matter what you believed."

"How about we compromise?" *A very husbandly thing to offer.* "Let's say I'm reformed, hmm?" Though to prove he hadn't completely left his wicked ways behind, Clarke claimed her mouth in a passionate kiss, bruising her soft lips with the force of his possession, and uncaring about being in full view of his mother and her companion.

Because this giant scoundrel got the woman of his dreams—a little sprite whose tender heart he'd forever protect.

EPILOGUE TWO

FIVE YEARS LATER

"**S**he looks like you, mama!"

Iris nodded at her daughter's correct assessment of the fairy painted in the book they were reading—one of Hazel's most popular sellers. "Indeed. Your mama was the inspiration for Aunt Hazel."

"Do you think she'll put me in a book, too?" Rowan's blonde waves practically vibrated with her excitement, and Iris couldn't help a chuckle at her child's enthusiasm.

A booming voice came from the doorway. "I don't see why not. Your aunt has no qualms about using whoever happens to float into her sphere for story ideas." Clarke held his arms out to catch Rowan as she leapt off the chaise and across the room. If Iris detected a note of annoyance in his tone, she ignored it, having given up trying to persuade him that *no, the grumpy black bear was not based on you*, knowing full well he most definitely was. Her sister enjoyed tormenting her brothers-in-law by inserting them in various tales, and Iris couldn't help the amusement she gained from it herself.

Clarke and Owen's reactions were especially priceless upon the big reveal, the entire family joining in the friendly ribbing.

"Can I send a letter to Aunt Hazel asking her to make me a fairy like mama?" Rowan tried wriggling from her father's grasp, unwilling to wait for an answer before racing upstairs, calling for her favorite maid to bring writing supplies. No doubt the precocious child would be dictating several letters before landing on the perfect one to mail to Manchester.

"You two get fairies while I get a grumpy old bear. Your sister has it out for me, I swear." Clarke sat by her and wrapped an arm around her shoulders, pulling Iris closer.

"Along with her other two brothers-in-law. Don't forget them. I actually think Owen has it worse than you... Who wants to be a slug?" Her nose wrinkled at the thought as she cuddled deeper into her husband's warm embrace. The familiar scent of lemongrass tickled her nose, and she allowed the tart aroma to ease her mind and muscles after a long day of playing with Rowan and managing the household.

"Valid point. Bears trump slugs any day." Clarke's hand stroked the side of her neck, playing with a loose strand of hair. "How was your day, sprite? The little one wasn't too much trouble, was she?"

"Hardly. Her energy is reminiscent of when my sisters and I ran about Shoreham. She exudes the same vigor and sass, which is a comforting reminder of our happy childhood."

And now Iris lived as happily as an adult with her husband and daughter. She never did write Linton about them expecting a baby, though it didn't matter in the end. The marquess died a month before Rowan was born. An innkeeper found him lying prone on the ground from a knife wound, and the call for a doctor had been too late.

She suspected foul play, possibly repayment for a debt, but no one was certain. The news pained Iris, but it didn't match the same grief she felt when Mama and Papa passed away. Linton never let her fully love him, and he certainly didn't care for her—so Iris's feelings were as they would be for any acquaintance who met their end too early. Sad but ultimately able to move on with her life.

And what a life.

A handsome husband whom she adored.

A daughter who filled her heart with love and affection.

And every other member of her growing family who made her feel like she belonged, who crushed her past fears of being abandoned.

"What are you thinking about?" Clarke asked, studying her content expression.

"Just about how happy I am. How much I love you and our life. It's more than I ever dared dream." That's one thing she could thank Linton for—he'd brought the two of them together.

And that's enough.

THE END

THANK YOU FOR READING!

Please consider leaving a rating/review. Ratings & reviews are the #1 way to support an indie author like me.

They don't have to be long or even positive (though I hope you enjoyed this book!). All the algorithms care about are QUANTITY.

The more reviews, the more my books are shown to other potential readers!

And they serve as guides to readers on whether or not to take a chance on an indie author.

To stay up-to-date on new releases and more, join my newsletter, and follow me on Instagram: @authorjemmafrost!

I appreciate your support!

Happy Reading,

Jemma

ALSO BY JEMMA FROST

Charming Dr. Forrester
All Rogues Lead to Ruin
An Earl Like Any Other
The Scoundrel Seeks a Wife
A Gentleman Never Surrenders

ABOUT THE AUTHOR

J emma Frost grew up in the Midwest where she visited the library every day and read romance novels voraciously! Now, she lives in North Carolina with her cat, Spencer, and dreams of stories to be written!

FOLLOW JEMMA FROST on Instagram and/or Facebook: @authorjemmafrost